FILE UNDER:
13 SUSPICIOUS INCIDENTS

LEMONY SNICKET

ART BY SETH

Little, Brown and Company
New York Boston

Little, Brown and Company

Hachette Book Group
237 Park Avenue, New York, NY 10017
Visit our website at lb-kids.com

Little, Brown and Company is a division of Hachette Book Group, Inc.
The Little, Brown name and logo are trademarks of
Hachette Book Group, Inc.

The publisher is not responsible for websites (or their content)
that are not owned by the publisher.

First Edition: April 2014

Library of Congress Control Number: 2013037873

ISBN 978-0-316-28403-5 (hc) — ISBN 978-0-316-28406-6 (ebook edition no. 1) —
ISBN 978-0-316-28404-2 (ebook edition no. 2)

10 9 8 7 6 5 4 3 2 1

RRD-C

Printed in the United States of America

FILE UNDER:
13 SUSPICIOUS INCIDENTS

Please find enclosed herein thirteen (13) reports filed under "Suspicious Incidents" in our archives. The thirteen (13) reports have thirteen (13) conclusions which have been separated from their corresponding reports for security reasons. The reports are contained in sub-file One (1) and the conclusions in sub-file B (b) so that it is impossible for each report and conclusion to be in the same place at once. For your convenience, both sub-files are enclosed together in this bound volume.

The information contained herein is secret and important, meant only for members of our organization. If you are not a member of our organization, please put this down, as it is neither secret nor important and therefore will not interest you.

All misfiled information, by definition, is none of your business.

Sub-file One:
REPORTS.

Inside Job. Pinched Creature. Ransom Note. Walkie-Talkie. Bad Gang. Silver Spoon. Violent Butcher. Twelve or Thirteen. Midnight Demon. Three Suspects. Vanished Message. Troublesome Ghost. Figure in Fog.

INSIDE JOB.

One morning I was arguing with the adult in charge of me. I'm sure I don't have to tell you what that is like, and it is one of the world's great difficulties that this sort of argument goes on nearly every place on almost every morning between practically every child and some adult or other. Another one of the world's great difficulties was S. Theodora Markson. During my time in Stain'd-by-the-Sea, Theodora was my chaperone and I was her apprentice. Being her apprentice meant that we shared a small room in a hotel called the Lost Arms. The room was too small to share with one of the world's great difficulties, and this was probably why we were arguing.

"Lemony Snicket," she was saying to me, "tell me exactly what being an apprentice means."

"S. Theodora Markson," I said, "tell me exactly what the *S* stands for in your name."

"Snide answers aren't proper," she said. "They're not sensible."

"I know it," I said, and I did. "Snide" is a word which here means "the kind of tone you use in an argument," and "sensible" refers to the tone you are supposed to use instead.

"If you're smart enough to know that," Theodora said, snidely, "then tell me all about being an apprentice."

"You and I are in a secret organization," I began, but Theodora looked wildly around the room and shook her head at me. My chaperone's hair was a crazed and woolly mess, so when she looked around the room and shook her head, it was like seeing something go wrong at a mop factory.

"Shush!" she hissed.

"Why shush?"

"You know why shush. You shouldn't talk about our secret organization. You shouldn't even say the words 'secret organization' out loud."

"You've just said them twice."

"It doesn't count if I say it in order to tell you not to say it."

"Well, what can I say instead?"

"You know what."

"No, I don't know what," I said. "That's why I asked you."

"Say 'you know what,'" Theodora said, "instead of 'secret organization.' That way you won't have to say 'secret organization' out loud, which you should never do."

"Except in order to tell me not to say it," I reminded her, and went on with my answer. "You and I are in you know what, and being your

3

apprentice means I'm learning all the methods and techniques used by you know what. There are sinister plots afoot in this town, and you and I should be working together to defeat them in the name of you know what."

"Wrong," Theodora said, with a stern hair-shake. "Being my apprentice means you do everything I say."

"That's not what I was told," I said.

"Who told you?"

"You know who," I said, just to be safe, "at you know what, you know where, when, and how."

"You're talking nonsense," Theodora said. "Breakfast is ready. As your chaperone, I'm telling you to hand me two napkins."

"As your apprentice," I said, "I'm telling you we don't have any."

"I suppose it doesn't matter," Theodora said, and I suppose she was right. My chaperone made us breakfast every morning on a metal plate provided by the Lost Arms. When you flicked a switch the plate got hot, and this morning Theodora had laid two slices of bread on it and then begun arguing with me. Now the bread was burned black on one side, like a shingle covered in tar, and the other side was soft and cold from sitting on the windowsill we used as a refrigerator. A napkin would not turn a half-burned, half-cold piece of bread into breakfast. A garbage bin would have been more helpful. I put the failed toast in my mouth anyway. Theodora didn't think it was proper for her apprentice to talk with his mouth full, so it was the best way to avoid talking to her.

Over the sound of burned crusts against my teeth I heard a knock on the door, and Prosper Lost peeked in at us. He was the Lost Arms' proprietor, a word which here means he stood around the lobby with a small smile and called it running the place. I called it a little creepy, although not to his face. "Lemony Snicket," he said.

"You're not Lemony Snicket," Theodora said to him.

"There's someone downstairs to see you," Lost explained to me.

Theodora frowned at the proprietor. "Whoever's waiting downstairs isn't Lemony Snicket either," she said. "Lemony Snicket is right here with crumbs on his shirt."

"Someone is here to see Lemony Snicket," Prosper Lost said, as clearly as he could.

"Thank you," I told the proprietor, and excused myself.

"Whatever you're doing," Theodora called after me, "be quick about it. You have a very busy day, Snicket. You have to buy some napkins."

My mouth wasn't full, but I pretended it was so I didn't have to answer as Prosper Lost led me down the stairs. "Who is it who wants to see me?" I asked him.

"A minor," Lost replied.

"Do you mean a child, or someone who works in a mine?"

"Both," Lost said, and sure enough, in the

lobby was a girl about my age wearing a helmet with a light attached to it, the kind people wear when digging underground. The hat looked a little big on her head, and she took off some over-sized work gloves so she could shake my hand.

"I'm Marguerite Gracq," she said. "I spell it in the French way."

"I'm Lemony Snicket," I said. "I think my name is spelled the same in any language."

"Around town they say you're something of a detective."

"Around town they're wrong. I'm something else."

"Well, I need some help."

"What kind of help?"

"Pictures are falling down in my living room."

"Sounds like you need a handyman."

Marguerite shook her head. "They're falling too neatly."

"Maybe it's just because I've had a lousy

breakfast," I told her, "but I'm not following you."

"Follow me to my home," Marguerite said, "and I'll explain everything and poach you an egg, besides. I put a little vinegar in the poaching water, so my eggs turn out nice and fluffy."

A fluffy poached egg is a good breakfast, and a good breakfast is better than a bad one, like a good book is better than having your toe chopped off. We walked out of the Lost Arms together and down the quiet street. Most of the streets in Stain'd-by-the-Sea were quiet. The town was emptying out.

"I know that most businesses in town have been failing," I told Marguerite, with a nod at a boarded-up shop. "How's mining going?"

"There's just one small mine in Stain'd-by-the-Sea," she said, "and it's in my front yard. My father says we've gotten all the gold we're going to get from it. He's out of town for a few weeks finding us a better place to live. I'm staying here to close up the mine and make sure nothing happens to the gold."

"He left you here all alone?"

Marguerite frowned and shook her head. "He hired a woman named Dagmar to watch over me. She doesn't do much but sit and listen to the radio. I don't like her."

"What does she listen to?"

"Polkas."

"No wonder you don't like her."

Marguerite smiled. "That's not the only reason," she said. "Dagmar doesn't seem trustworthy. The paintings didn't start falling until she arrived, and nobody else has been around. I keep thinking she's after something, but nothing has been stolen."

"Most untrustworthy people hanging around a gold mine are after the gold."

"My father has been very careful about his stash," she said. "When we bring gold up from the mine, he immediately takes it all to his workshop

9

to melt it down. Then he hides it someplace in that room. Even I don't know exactly where, and I have the only workshop key. My father gave it to me when he left town, and I keep it with me always."

Marguerite reached into her overalls and drew out a skinny key on a thick cord around her neck.

"Have you ever let Dagmar use the key?" I asked. "She could have had a copy made."

Marguerite shook her head. "I'm the only one who's been in the workshop since my father left, and I can see that nothing has been touched. The problem's not with the gold, Snicket. It's with the pictures in my living room."

We'd arrived at a small wooden house with a roof covered in moss, narrow windows wide open, and a large hole in the front yard with the top of a ladder jutting out from it. Various tools were scattered around the browning lawn. From the windows I could hear a particularly peppy polka. All polka music is peppy. There's nothing

wrong with feeling peppy, but a polka insists that everyone else has to be peppy too, even if they don't feel like it.

Marguerite kicked off her boots and led me into a friendly-looking place. There was a large wooden staircase with piles of books here and there, and a carpet decorated with images of mythical beasts and smudges of dirt. Leafy plants hung in the windows, shedding leaves wherever I looked.

"I'm back, Dagmar," Marguerite called upstairs. "I have a friend with me! I'm going to make him a poached egg!"

"Do whatever you want," replied a cranky voice, over the sound of the polka. The music's peppiness had clearly not spread to Dagmar.

"The kitchen's right over here," Marguerite said, "but if you don't mind, I'd like to show you the living room first."

"Of course," I said, and she led me through an archway into a room as pleasant and rumpled as the rest of the house. The wooden floor was painted black, with the paint peeling off here and there, and the sofas and chairs were all bright yellow except where they were patched up with squares of other bright fabrics. There was a large reading lamp, made from another miner's helmet, and on the walls were portraits of pale, thoughtful-looking people, with one portrait leaning against the wall underneath a blank space on the wall where it clearly belonged. One portrait, depicting a man with a bow tie and an elegant cane, had a large rip right across the middle, and Marguerite looked at it sadly. "Henry Parland was the first one to fall," she said, "just a few minutes after Dagmar arrived. Luckily, it's the only one that's been damaged. Since then, it seems that one falls whenever I'm down in the mine. Paavo Cajander, Katri Vala, Eino Leino, Otto Manninen, and this morning Larin Paraske, who had already fallen, was found right as you see her, leaning on the wall like all the others."

"Your father certainly likes Finnish poets," I said.

"These portraits belonged to my mother," Marguerite said. "They were precious to her, but they're not particularly valuable."

"And they haven't particularly been taken," I said.

"Nothing has," Marguerite said, looking around the room. "I admit I'm suspicious of Dagmar, but I can't say she's committed any kind of crime. The paintings just keep falling and then we hang them back up."

"You say they fall when you're in the mine," I said, glancing out the window at the hole in the yard, "but surely you can't hear them fall from down there."

"Dagmar tells me they've fallen," Marguerite said, "or I notice myself when I come in for a snack."

"And who puts them back up?"

"I do," Marguerite said, with a note of pride in

her voice. "I fetch a hammer and a nail from the workshop and do the job myself. And I do it right, Snicket. Don't think it's my fault they keep falling."

"Maybe the first one fell," I said, with a glance at the rip in Henry Parland, "but if the others were found leaning against the wall like this, they probably didn't fall."

"That's how they were," Marguerite said with a nod. "Leaning against the wall, nice and neat, with nothing damaged."

"Do you leave the workshop door open while you rehang them?"

Marguerite gave me a sharp look. "Of course not. The gold is somewhere in that room, and it's my responsibility to keep it locked up."

I turned my eyes from the girl to Larin Paraske. The poet in the portrait looked back at me but offered nothing more than a thoughtful gaze and an unusual hat. I tilted the portrait and looked behind it at the cord stretched across so the painting would hang evenly from the nail. I looked at the blank space on the wall, and at the tiny hole in the dark wood. "Do you have a lot of nails in the workshop?" I asked.

"Jars and jars full," Marguerite said. "My father uses these special black nails all around the house. They curve slightly, so they do less damage to the wall."

"And what about the hammer?"

"It's an ordinary enough hammer," Marguerite said. "Do you want to see it?"

"I don't need to," I said. "I'm going upstairs to talk to Dagmar."

"What are you going to ask her?"

"First," I said, "I'll ask her to turn off that blasted polka music. And then I'll demand that she return all she's stolen from your family, before we hand her over to the police."

• • •

The conclusion to "Inside Job" is filed under "Black Paint," page 209.

PINCHED CREATURE.

I was spending the afternoon with my associate Moxie Mallahan. Moxie was Stain'd-by-the-Sea's only reporter, a job she had learned from her parents, who had run the town's newspaper, *The Stain'd Lighthouse*. The newspaper was shut down, Mrs. Mallahan had left town, Mr. Mallahan was sleeping late, and Moxie and I were just hanging around the lighthouse, doing a little reading and talking over various incidents that had happened recently. "It's been too long since we've done this," Moxie said.

"Done what?"

"Had an uneventful time like this."

Right on cue, the doorbell rang, as if to say enough was enough of uneventfulness, and when Moxie opened the door, there was an event. The event was a boy several years younger than I was and much more upset. He wore a white coat like a scientist and had two pairs of glasses, one over his eyes and the other perched on his head.

"I'm sorry to disturb you," the boy said, "but you're the closest neighbor and I need some help."

"Oliver," Moxie said. "I didn't know your family was still in town." She turned to me. "Oliver's parents are the only veterinarians left in Stain'd-by-the-Sea. So few people have pets nowadays, I'd assumed the Doctors Sobol had closed up shop."

"They have," Oliver said, his eyes blinking nervously behind his glasses, "but I'm here for a few more months running the business until they come and fetch me."

"Well, if you ever want company," Moxie said, "hike up the hill and we'll play some Parcheesi. This is my friend Lemony Snicket, by the way. He won't play Parcheesi because he says it's inane."

"It *is* inane," I said, "and inane is a word which here means pointless and dull."

Oliver frowned, and I can't say I blame him. If you are worried about something, it is not a good time to listen to people argue over games and vocabulary. He sat down glumly at the bottom of the stairs that spiraled up to the lighthouse's lantern.

"I'm sorry, Oliver," Moxie said. "We were prattling on while you have something on your mind."

"I sure do," Oliver said. "I've lost a newt."

Moxie and I both looked at Oliver. If we'd looked at each other we might have laughed.

"It might sound silly," Oliver said, "but this newt is very important."

Moxie's eyebrows went up underneath her hat. "What could be so important about a little lizard?"

"First of all," Oliver said, "newts aren't lizards. A lizard is a reptile, and a newt is an amphibian. Second of all, this newt is a very rare subspecies. I've lost an Amaranthine Newt, known for its bright yellow color and prevalent left-handedness. It was the only one in captivity and prized by herpetologists and southpaws all over the world."

"Why do they call it the Amaranthine Newt, if it's bright yellow?" I asked. "Amaranthine means purple, doesn't it?"

"Its eggs are purple," Oliver said. "My father took the eggs with him to his new job at Amphibians-A-Go-Go, an aquatic animal center and amusement park just outside the city. The newt and I are supposed to join them there soon. If I can't find the newt, my father might lose his job."

"Don't fret, Oliver," Moxie said, although I could see that Oliver just kept on fretting. "Snicket here has a knack for finding strange missing items. Isn't that so, Snicket?"

"It's sometimes so," I said. "Oliver, why don't you tell us how the newt slipped away?"

"I don't think it slipped away," Oliver said. "I think it was pinched."

"Somebody stole it?" Moxie said. "That's a serious accusation to make." She sat down and opened a case sitting on the floor. Inside was a typewriter that Moxie Mallahan always kept nearby, and she started taking notes immediately on the clattering machine.

"I'm making it seriously," Oliver said. "The Amaranthine Newt lives in a special tank on a desk in my examining room, so I can always keep an eye on it. It was there when I opened for business this morning."

"And how many patients did you have today?" I asked.

"Just one," Oliver said. "You were right about few people having pets, Moxie, but Polly Partial has two of the last cats in town, and one of them has a narcissistic disorder."

"Polly Partial, the grocer?" Moxie asked, and met my eye. Neither of us was fond of the woman who ran Partial Foods, but lots of people nobody is fond of have sick cats.

"Her cat Paperbag has been a patient of my family's for a very long time," Oliver said. "I can't imagine that his owner is a thief, but greed and newts can do strange things to people. I examined Paperbag and went to my desk to write out a prescription. Then I escorted Partial and Paperbag out and spent a few minutes in the backyard watering my father's zinnias. The flowers match the trim on the office, as long as you keep them healthy, and I'd like to leave the place looking nice. When I went back into the office, the tank was empty."

"Someone must have snuck in while you were gardening," Moxie said.

Oliver shook his head. "I would have heard anyone else driving up the road."

"They need not have arrived by automobile," I said.

"To pinch my newt," Oliver said, "they'd need a similar tank. You couldn't fit one on a bicycle or a donkey. Polly Partial must have stolen the newt, but I don't see how."

"I don't mean to be rude," I said, "but can you really trust your eyes? I notice you have not one but two pairs of glasses."

Oliver gave me a stern, lens-covered look. "My eyes aren't perfect," he said, "but with these glasses I can see perfectly well, and I keep the other pair on my head for reading."

"You don't have bifocals?" I asked, referring to eyeglasses that combine two lenses into one.

"There aren't any optometrists left in town," Moxie told me. "The closest eye doctor is way over in Paltryville, but she doesn't have a very good reputation."

"Did you use your reading glasses when you were with Paperbag?" I asked Oliver.

He nodded. "When I wrote out the prescription."

"Well, I'm sure you saw clearly," I said, "but I'm not sure I do. Shall we walk over to the Sobol office?"

Oliver said yes and so we did, Moxie carrying her typewriter and me trying to think. It was a warm, breezy day, with the wind carrying a salty smell from the seaweed of the Clusterous Forest, an eerie phenomenon that lay below the cliff we were on. But we walked the other way, down a road as bumpy and cracked as a vase falling down stairs. Soon enough, we could see the office of the Doctors Sobol, a faraway building with yellow and orange trim, but when we rounded a corner, something made us stop. There was a car, pulled over to the side of the road, and a man frowning at the car like it'd given him socks for his birthday.

"Good afternoon," I said.

"Not in my opinion," the man replied, and used his right hand to point at one of the car's tires. It also looked a little sad. "I seem to have a flat."

"There's a garage about a half mile thataway," Moxie said, pointing thataway with one finger.

"Thank you," the man said. "I'm a doorknob salesman passing through town, and I'm late for an appointment. I guess I'd better walk on over to the garage. My car doesn't have anything valuable in it, so I suppose it will be all right."

I peeked through the window of his car. I couldn't help it. I've been trained to do such things. There was nothing in it.

Oliver had other concerns. "You haven't noticed a newt crawling around, have you?"

"Or a suspicious person?" Moxie added.

"What kind of person?" the man asked. "I

saw a woman driving by in a beat-up grocery van. And what kind of lizard?"

Oliver sighed in annoyance. "It's an Amaranthine Newt," he said, "and that woman is probably a thief."

"A newt will be hard to find," said the stranger. "But I might look in a patch of zinnias I passed. It could blend in and hide there easily."

"You're thinking of a chameleon," I said, "but you're probably right that we won't find the newt. We might as well help you instead."

"What?" Oliver said, blinking in astonishment, and Moxie frowned.

"Do you have a spare tire in the trunk?" I continued, talking to the man.

The supposed salesman shook his head. "Nope."

"That's too bad," I said, "but maybe you have something that would do in a pinch."

"I don't think so," the man said quickly, in a pinched voice.

"In a pinch" is a phrase which here means "in a difficult situation," and a pinched voice is a whiny and nervous one. But neither of these pinches was the pinch I was thinking of. "Open the trunk anyway," I said, "so we can see the special newt tank you have hidden there."

• • •

The conclusion to "Pinched Creature" is filed under "Dishonest Salesman," page 213.

RANSOM NOTE.

Bouvard and Pecuchet Bellerophon, better known as Pip and Squeak, were the best cabdrivers in Stain'd-by-the-Sea, although to be fair, they were also the only cabdrivers I'd ever come across in town. The brothers weren't really old enough to drive—or tall enough, for that matter—so Pip worked the steering wheel and Squeak worked the brakes, and in this way they got their customers around in the taxi belonging to their father, who they'd told me was very ill. The Bellerophon brothers were valuable associates of mine, so when they told me their mechanic needed help, I agreed to ride right over to Moray Wheels, a dirty and lonely-looking garage in what had once been a bustling district of town and now sat mostly empty.

"I know it doesn't look like much," Pip said as his brother brought the taxi to a halt, "but Jackie's an excellent mechanic."

"You can say that again," Squeak said, in his high-pitched voice, but nobody did. We were busy watching an elderly man wander out onto the driveway with a limp and a sneer. He wobbled slightly as he walked and his fingers fluttered at his sides like he was counting to infinity on his fingers.

"That's the mechanic?" I asked doubtfully, imagining those fingers trying to operate a wrench.

"*That*," Pip said, with a shake of his head, "is the mechanic's grandfather. Wednesdays he works at the bowling alley, but the rest of the time he sits around here eating molasses and bragging about his career as a race car driver. Jackie's probably inside. Let's go."

Let's go we did. The brothers led me in a curve around the old man and then into a garage that felt like a birthday party for mechanical parts, with tires and bumpers drinking gasoline punch, and stacks of tools and equipment nibbling on grease and talking together on the floor. There was no sign of Jackie or anyone else, but in the middle of the place was a car I recognized.

"What's wrong with Cleo Knight's Dilemma?" I asked. "Ms. Knight is an associate of mine, and her automobile has always been top-of-the-line. You wouldn't believe some of the stunts that car has pulled."

A figure rolled itself out from under the shiny automobile, and someone about my age sat up and nodded at all of us. "Even something top-of-the-line bottoms out once in a while," the mechanic said. "She just needs a little tune-up, that's all. Is this the guy, brothers?"

"This is the guy," Squeak squeaked.

Jackie gave me a quick, frowny glance. "He doesn't look so tough."

"He's plenty tough," Pip said.

"I need someone *very* tough," Jackie said.

"Do you need someone who can hear what you say, even when he's standing right here?" I asked.

Jackie gave me an apologetic smile. "It's nothing personal," the mechanic said. "I just have some trouble on my hands."

"Trouble is like grease," I said, with a nod at Jackie's jumpsuit. "If you have it on you, you'll probably get it on everyone nearby."

"Pip and Squeak said you're good in a jam," Jackie said.

"Depends on the jam," I said.

"They say you're brave."

"Brave is what they call you until it doesn't

work," I said. "Then they call you beaten. But you don't want to hear my story. You want to tell me yours."

Jackie sighed and sat down on a stack of tires. "My dog's gone."

Squeak gasped. "Not Lysistrata? She's the best watchdog I've ever seen!"

"Loudest bark this side of the Mortmain Mountains," Jackie said with pride, "but someone swiped her last night, and left this note for me taped to the Dilemma's windshield."

The mechanic took a sheet of paper out of a dirty pocket, and we all leaned in to see.

If you ever want to see your dog alive again, bring a complete set of Dugga Drills to 1300 Blotted Boulevard at midnight tonight. Be sensible. Come alone.

> *Yours sincerely,*
> *The Person Who Kidnapped*
> *Your Dog*

"Dugga makes the best drills money can buy," Jackie said, "but I'd give anything to have my dog back."

"Who knows you have such valuable tools?" I asked.

The mechanic pointed to a corner, where there was a bright red case marked DUGGA. "Anyone who comes by," Jackie said. "But what I can't figure is how a stranger got my Lysistrata to come with them, and where they're hiding her now. She'd be barking like crazy, but I rode around all morning and heard nothing."

"Did you go by the Hairdryer Emporium?" Pip asked. "That's probably the loudest place in Stain'd-by-the-Sea. The kidnapper could be hiding her there."

"I'm not from around here," I reminded the Bellerophons. "Who runs the Hairdryer Emporium?"

"Hal Hairdryer," said Squeak. "You've probably seen him out in front of his brother's place,

Hairdryer's Salamis. He has a funny hat and two very serious arms."

"But that place closed up a couple of weeks ago," Jackie said, and sighed. "If he's the kidnapper, I don't know where we'd find him."

"Running a loud business isn't reason enough to call him a kidnapper," I said. "The best way to find out who took Lysistrata is to catch them red-handed when you bring them the ransom."

"Will you come with me tonight, Snicket?" The mechanic gestured to a motorcycle waiting by the door. "I'll put the drills in the saddlebag and pick you up at the Lost Arms around eleven. We'll get there early and you can hide yourself. That way we can get my dog back *and* catch whoever did it."

"Blotted Boulevard will sure be spooky at that hour," Pip said, reminding me of a time we'd been out there together, chasing a villain named Hangfire. "We'll come with you, too."

"No," Jackie said. "The kidnappers would notice your taxi. The note said to come alone."

I looked at the note again. "Be sensible" was something my chaperone, Theodora, said all the time, but like the case of Dugga Drills, this was something plenty of people had noticed.

"You kids get outta here!" The voice came from the doorway, where Jackie's grandfather was leaning with a jar of molasses in one hand, and, in the other, a jar of molasses. His voice was sticky and slurry, because his mouth was either full of molasses or empty of teeth, or both.

"They're friends, Grampa," Jackie said.

"They're keeping you from your work," the old man said, spitting a brown glop onto the floor. "That Knight girl's going to get very impatient."

"I've told you a thousand times," Jackie said. "You're not going to take over this job for me."

"You could at least let me deliver it," slurred the old man. "That car deserves to have a driver like me. After all, I competed in the Magritte Derby."

"That was thirty-seven years ago," Jackie

said patiently, "and you came in thirty-eighth. I'll deliver it myself, thank you."

"You can't drive a Dilemma. You don't have the reflexes of a professional like me."

"Your hands shake from too much sugar," Jackie said, "and your ears ring constantly from the bowling alley."

"I like ringing ears!" the old man cried.

It is better to dive into a shark tank than into a family argument. "We'd best get going," I said. "See you later, Jackie."

"Much obliged," Jackie replied, which is a fancy way of saying "thank you," and slid back under the equally fancy car.

It was not easy to persuade my chaperone to let me help Jackie get Lysistrata back, but I explained it to her in a whisper at about ten thirty that night, when Theodora had fallen asleep, and I took her silence to be words which here mean "Go ahead, Snicket. Sneak out without waking me, and take a motorcycle ride in the middle of the night."

I gave Prosper Lost a wave as I headed out, and Jackie was waiting with an extra helmet and a grim expression.

"I took the long way here, just to see if I could hear my dog barking anyplace."

"The kidnapper could have drugged her," I said, thinking of Hangfire again.

The mechanic shuddered. "I just can't imagine who would kidnap my dog, even to get a set of expensive drills as ransom."

"They could have stolen those drills," I said, "when they stole the dog."

"Lysistrata would have barked at any intruder," Jackie said, "and I would have awoken."

It wasn't a bad answer, but it wasn't good enough, just like my list of suspects. Hangfire was associated with Blotted Boulevard. Hal Hairdryer ran a loud establishment suitable for hiding a loud dog. Theodora liked the word "sensible." Not a bad list, but it didn't feel good enough.

I probably do not need to tell you that young

people should not be riding around on motor-
cycles, even if the driver is a skilled mechanic
with an extra helmet, and even if there's a sort
of magical terror to feeling the night air rushing
in your face and the engine whining underneath
you. I hung on tight to Jackie's shoulders and
tried to decide if I was more scared than excited
or more excited than scared. I decided it was a tie.

We arrived early at Blotted Boulevard, as
planned, and stood for a moment together on the
silent, empty block. I hid behind a pile of rubble
that looked like it had once been a newsstand, and
Jackie stood beneath a flickering streetlight and
waited. I waited, too. We kept waiting and then
we kept at it. Both of us waited for almost two
hours. Even in my hiding place I felt like a target,
or an animal soon to become prey. I don't know
what Jackie felt like, out there where anyone
could see. But if anyone saw, nobody came forward. We spent two late hours waiting for nothing, and finally the mechanic came to fetch me.

"Nobody showed," Jackie said.

"I thought nobody would," I admitted, "but it didn't hurt to be sure."

"Well, you're a good sport to help me," Jackie said. "I'll take you back to your hotel."

I shook my head. "Let's ride around for a while," I said.

Jackie smiled. "You like a joyride?"

"Joyride" is a word for driving around just for fun, but I'd had enough excitement for one evening and said so. "But joyriding is the whole reason for your dog's disappearance. I think the kidnapper's had his fun by now, and I'm sure Lysistrata will be returned to you."

•   •   •

The conclusion to "Ransom Note" is filed under "Loud Dog," page 217.

WALKIE-TALKIE.

I was at the counter at Hungry's finishing a lunch Jake Hix had been kind enough to fix me. It was a mess of spaghetti tossed together with some spinach, a little cheese, and a chopped-up onion burned almost to a crisp, with a perfect fried egg on top of it. He called it a name I couldn't remember, something he'd learned from an unemployed gondolier who had passed through town. I called it almost perfect. It would have been more than almost perfect had there been better company at the counter. On one side was a lean man in a green suit and a hat with a feather on it, but he wasn't who the problem was.

Stew Mitchum was on the other side. Think of something noble and true, like a librarian or a good crisp apple or a sweater that doesn't itch, and then think of the opposite, and that's Stew Mitchum. He was a rat and a nuisance and many other troublesome words I knew, the sort of person who might dump a whole shaker on your head if you asked him to pass the salt. A little salt on my egg would have been good, but I didn't risk it. Stew was having lunch, too—three chocolate muffins at full price, and he was trying to bargain his way to a fourth.

"No way, Fay Wray," Hix said to Stew, using one of his favorite expressions. "I'm cutting you off. Three chocolate muffins are your limit."

"Be a sport, Jake," Stew said, in a whiny tone that never gets anyone to be a sport.

"I don't like sports except croquet and water

polo," Jake said, "and I don't like you except you're a paying customer. You don't have enough money for a fourth muffin, and if you eat any more sugar you'll be so shaky you'll drop crumbs on my nice clean floor."

"I'll pay you double tomorrow."

"You can pay me triple yesterday. The answer is no."

"I could call the cops on you."

Jake sighed and pointed at Stew. "First of all, call them your parents, because that's who the only cops are in Stain'd-by-the-Sea. And secondly, denying you a fourth muffin isn't a crime. I'd call it a mercy."

Stew's face snarled up like elevator doors had closed on it. "Then maybe I won't pay for the first three," he said.

"You already did."

"Well, maybe I won't leave a tip. Think it over while I use the can." With that rude phrase I've never liked, Stew slid off the stool and clattered away to the door marked RESTROOMS, and the man in the green suit frowned after him.

"What was that all about?" he asked.

"That's about four and a half feet tall and about as nice as a wasp stuck indoors," Hix told him. "More coffee?"

"No, thank you," the man said, and left a few bills on the counter. "Keep the change and keep out of trouble. I should be back in town next month."

He nodded at both of us, the feather on his hat nodding, too, and off he went. Jake fed the money to the cash register and wiped the counter clean. "Been meaning to tell you, Snicket," Jake said. "I'm trying one of those books you recommended about the clever kid in Utah. Don't squawk but so far I'm not liking it much."

My mouth was full of crunchy onion, but Hix frowned at me. "I said don't squawk," he said.

"I didn't squawk," I told him, after I'd swallowed.

"Someone squawked, I heard it," he said, and then I heard it too. For a minute I thought there was a radio in my shoe, as had once been required as part of my education. But the squawking sound came from the floor, and it was followed by a cry for help.

"What was that?" Jake asked.

"Help! Help!" the voice called again, and in moments I was crouching on the floor next to the counter. As Jake had mentioned, it was a nice clean floor, so it was easy to find what I was looking for. The squawking object was small and black, with an on-off switch, a round speaker, a red button marked TALK, and a piece of tape with more letters I couldn't make sense of.

"Help! Help!" said the object again.

"It's a walkie-talkie," I said, and pressed the red button. "Lemony Snicket here. Can I be of assistance? Over."

I'd remembered to say "over," a word which when spoken on a walkie-talkie means "I'm done talking and it's your turn," a code that the person on the matching walkie-talkie sounded too panicked to remember. "Help!" it said, so crackly I could not even tell if the voice belonged to a man or a woman. "Where's George? George, help me!"

Jake looked at the walkie-talkie and then at the door. "My customer!" he said. "He must have dropped it."

"Is his name George?"

"I don't know," Jake said. "I just know him as the guy who comes into town once a month for steak frites."

"Can you hear me?" the voice asked, and I pressed the red button again.

"I can hear you," I said, and headed toward the door. Jake took off his apron and followed. Steak frites is nothing more than a steak with French fries, but it's delicious if it's done well. I tried to be good at my job, too. "What is the nature of your emergency? Over."

"I'm trapped, over," said the voice. "I need

George to rescue me. Over. Our enemies have captured me."

There was a moment of staticky silence from the walkie-talkie as Jake and I stepped outside. Down the block I saw just a glimpse of a figure turning the corner, too quick for me to see if it was the man in the green suit, but Jake and I looked at each other and headed in that direction.

"George?" said the walkie-talkie.

"We're trying to find him for you," I said. "Over."

"Help me! Over! Help me!"

"Tell me more about your situation, over," I said, halfway down the block.

There was another silence from the walkie-talkie, and I looked at the piece of tape and the letters printed there.

OFF-SBTS-USE

It was no word I'd heard of. The closest I could think of was "obtuse," which could refer to a large angle or a dim-witted person, but "obtuse" didn't have dashes in the middle. Not many words or phrases did, but maybe in a dashy town like Stain'd-by-the-Sea it was more common. Off-something, I thought. Perhaps it was just instructions to turn off the walkie-talkie.

"George and I," said the crackly voice, "are spies, and I have been captured."

"Is George wearing a green suit?" I asked, just as we reached the corner.

"How do I know?" the voice asked. "I'm miles away." The voice started to say something else, but then through the speaker I could hear a loud *whoosh* that interrupted. The noise reminded me of something I'd heard before, but I couldn't think what.

"What's happening?' I asked. "Over."

There was a brief pause, and then the voice grew louder and more worried. "Um, it's a flood!" it cried. "They're flooding the room!"

"George?" Jake called as we rounded the

corner, but there was no one but us on the sidewalk. I was thinking of the noise, like a waterfall but indoors.

"Help!" the voice said again, and out of a doorway stepped the man in the green suit.

"What's going on?" he asked. "I heard shouting just as I was entering my condominium."

"Are you George?" I asked him.

"No," the man said. "The name's Leroy."

Jake's face fell. "Are you *sure* you aren't George?"

"Are you obtuse?" the man said. "I'm quite sure of my name, thank you very much."

"Help!" the voice cried from the walkie-talkie. "Over! Find George!"

"We're sorry to have bothered you, sir," I said, and led Jake back the way we had come. The man disappeared from the street, and I pressed the button and said, "We're trying to find George. Is there anything else you can tell us about him? Over."

"He's a spy like I am," the voice said, after a short pause. "He might be in disguise, because of being a spy."

Jake and I looked at each other and then began to walk back toward Hungry's. I scanned the block and wondered if George could disguise himself as a streetlight, or the rind of a melon someone had tossed into the gutter. DRAIN-LEADS-TO-SEA, it said on the curb, and even though the sea was gone, I looked at the printing carefully.

"Does this label mean anything to you?" I asked Jake, showing him the tape.

"OFF-SBTS-USE," Jake tried to say out loud, but his mouth stumbled in the middle. "Maybe it's initials?"

"Help! Help!" the voice said, even more garbled than before. I hoped the spy wasn't starting to drown. I had a list of ways I would prefer to die. Drowning was toward the bottom of the list. My top choice was "never."

At the door to Hungry's we stopped again, looking every which way. We couldn't know who we were looking for, but it didn't matter. With no one on the streets, there was no one to find.

"How many customers have you had today?" I asked Jake.

"Not very many," he said, "and none of them looked like spies."

"Good spies don't look like spies," I said, and the walkie-talkie crackled in my hand again.

"Don't just hang around the door!" the muffled voice said. "Help me! Over!"

I turned the walkie-talkie off and pushed open the door to the diner. Stew Mitchum was behind the counter with his mouth full of muffin number four.

"You scoundrel!" Jake said, gasping behind me. "You swindler! You rake! You snake in the grass!"

"Snake in the grass" is a phrase for a person without scruples, such as a boy who would pretend to be a person in danger just to steal a muffin. But it wasn't the phrase I was thinking of. I suddenly knew what OFF-SBTS-USE meant. I'd learned something—two things, really, if you included the *whoosh* sound. I'd already known that Stew was a scoundrel, a swindler, a rake, and a snake in the grass. But now I knew where he got the two walkie-talkies—the one behind his back, and the one in my hands. And at least I'd learned that the snake in the grass was good about washing his hands.

·　·　·

The conclusion to "Walkie-Talkie" is filed under "Through the Window," page 221.

BAD GANG.

This is an account of an eventful weekend I had unchaperoned. I was unchaperoned because S. Theodora Markson decided to leave one Thursday morning to visit her sister, who lived in a charming cottage out in the country with a beautiful garden and a darling teacup collection and no little boy underfoot to muck up everything and ruin their fun. That was me. I was going to stay by myself all weekend and not make any trouble and maybe she would bring me a teacup as a reward if I did.

"That's all right," I told her. "You don't have to steal your sister's teacups on my behalf."

Theodora glared at me and put her suitcase in the back of her roadster, which was parked crookedly in front of the Lost Arms. My chaperone drove around in a green car that was so dilapidated I was afraid it would fall apart every time someone touched it. "I expect you to be good and follow all the rules of our organization."

"It's against the rules of our organization for the chaperone to take a vacation and leave her apprentice all alone," I said.

"You sound like a person who doesn't want a brand-new teacup."

"Most people sound like that," I said, but Theodora just shook her head and put on the leather helmet she always wore when driving, which captured her wild hair about as well as a handkerchief would capture a swarm of eels. She was a curious sight, S. Theodora Markson. She always was, and I was always curious about her.

"What does the *S* stand for?" I asked, over the ragged sound of the engine.

"*What?*" she shouted back.

"*What does the* S *stand for in your name?*"

"*See you Sunday!*" she said, and puttered off. I watched her go and then waited a sensible amount of time in case she forgot something and had to come puttering back. She didn't. I went back up to my room, and I'm not ashamed to say I did a little dance. It was the sort of dance you do when you're finally alone in your room. It was a short dance, and I had plenty of time to head on over to the library and read as long as I liked.

That was Thursday.

●

The next morning I took a walk to the old-est neighborhood in Stain'd-by-the-Sea. I don't know what I was looking for. I was thinking about my biggest case, a mystery which had started long, long before I'd arrived in town. Most of the clues had vanished. I thought perhaps a good place to look was the town's first business district, which was a few blocks of buildings around a small paved courtyard. The buildings had once been very impressive and now looked only as if they had once been very impressive. Weeds had come through the cobblestones of the courtyard, pushing them aside like their turn was over, and little metal chairs where people had once sat and sipped drinks were now scattered and rusty.

I found something straightaway, but I'm sorry to report it was Harvey and Mimi Mitchum, Stain'd-by-the-Sea's only police officers and the sort of married couple who argued from the moment they woke up in the morning to the moment they fell asleep in the middle of some cranky sentence. They weren't very good police officers, but to be fair, it was probably because they didn't have enough time to do a good job. They were too busy arguing. This particular Mitchum argument was taking place in front of a shop window which had been shattered, leaving jagged fragments of glass everywhere on the sidewalk. According to the sign, the store was called Boards, and sure enough, the man waiting for the officers to stop arguing was holding a thick plank.

"And I'm telling you, Mimi," Harvey Mitchum was saying when I approached, "that he only *thought* he heard the heart beating in his room. It wasn't *actually* beating."

"You're wrong about that," Mimi said. "I read the story better than you did."

"You can't read something *better*, Mimi. That's absurd."

"Then why did you think the store was called Broads when we first got here?"

"I just glanced at the sign."

"It's because you were thinking about broads, that's why."

"Excuse me," I said, and everyone turned to look at me, although only the man holding the board wasn't glaring.

"Move along, Snicket," Harvey said sternly. "This is police business. The Big Bad Brick Gang has struck again."

"Who are the Big Bad Brick Gang?" I asked.

"Not that it's any of your business," Mimi said, "but the Big Bad Brick Gang is an anonymous group of vandals and other malcontents who strike in secret in the middle of the night, with clever strategy and bricks. We cannot know when they will strike next and no one will ever catch them, but the whole world knows the menace of the Big Bad Brick Gang."

"I've never heard of them," I said.

The Mitchums looked at each other as if they were a little embarrassed. "Confidentially," Harvey Mitchum said, using a word which here means "please don't tell anyone," "we hadn't heard of them until this morning."

"My son has mentioned them before," said the man with the board. "When we heard the crash in the middle of the night, he guessed it was the Big Bad Brick Gang who was responsible." He called into the shop through the shattered window. "Kevin!"

A boy about my age stepped forward, holding a board in each hand. "Tell the police," the man said. "Tell them what you've heard about this Big Bad Brick Gang."

"Not much," Kevin said. "Just that they're an anonymous group of vandals and other malcontents. Vandals are people who destroy property, and malcontents are people who are angry enough to do such things."

"My son has been telling me that we should get a weapon to keep the store safe from this gang," the man said, using the plank to gesture down the street. "He's always going on about fencing and swashbuckling and all the other nonsense he gets from pirate books. I've told him it's foolishness."

"It *is* foolishness," Mimi said. "Weapons would be of no help. We cannot know where they will strike next."

"Did they steal anything, or just break the window?" I asked.

"They stole a board," the shopkeeper said. "It's our bestselling model, and it looks like this. In fact, this might be it. It's hard to tell. But there was a board in the window we had on sale, and I think they took it after they threw the brick."

"I'm glad that's all they took," I said.

"Don't be glad," Harvey snapped. "The police force of Stain'd-by-the-Sea will do all we can for Boards. It's an Old family business."

"I'm Bob Old," the shopkeeper explained. "My family has run this business for years. I'm grateful that you came, Officers, but I'm not sure what the police can do."

"That's true," Harvey said. "No one will ever catch them."

"How do you know all this about the Big Bad

Brick Gang," I asked, "if you've never heard of them until today?"

Mimi reached into the pocket of her police uniform and handed me a wadded-up piece of paper. "This was wrapped around the brick," she said, and I uncrumpled the note and read what it said.

Hello there,

We are the Big Bad Brick Gang, an anonymous group of vandals and other malcontents who strike in secret in the middle of the night, with clever strategy and bricks. You cannot know when we will strike next and no one will ever catch us, but the whole world knows the menace of the Big Bad Brick Gang.

Yours truly,
The Big Bad Brick Gang

"Just because they wrote that no one will ever catch them," I said, "doesn't mean it's true."

"You see?" Harvey said to his wife. "You don't read very well."

"What this foolish kid said has nothing to do with how well I read," Mimi said, and Bob Old walked back into his store as the Mitchums started up arguing again. I decided to leave, too. Listening to adults argue was a waste of a perfectly good unchaperoned day. Instead, I found Moxie Mallahan and we played a dice game her mother had taught her. Moxie's father went to bed so early that she was unchaperoned most of the time. It was the sort of dice game you could play for money, but we didn't. If we had played for money I would have owed Moxie a fortune.

That was Friday.

●

I woke up early and had breakfast at Hungry's, but as soon as Jake Hix told me the news I left my frittata half-finished and hurried back to the old section of town. There was another shattered window and another shopkeeper out front. This time the sign read SWORDS, and this time the Mitchums were standing there arguing again, although this time they had their son, Stew, with them. Stew Mitchum was a nasty piece of work. Like a cactus, the best thing to do with him was ignore him, no matter how much he kept poking me.

"Here you are again," Harvey Mitchum said. "I'm beginning to think you're a member of the BBBG yourself."

I was already a member of an organization that sometimes struck in the middle of the night, but I saw no reason to volunteer that information to the Mitchums. "I heard they struck again," I said.

Mimi shook her head and kicked at a piece of glass. "A Distinguished family business," she said. "I can't believe the BBBG dared to strike here."

"I'm Muriel Distinguished," the shopkeeper explained to me, and she began to sweep up the broken glass.

"Was anything stolen?" I asked.

"Just one sword, which we had displayed in the window," Ms. Distinguished said.

"Similar crime, similar note," Harvey said, waving a piece of paper.

Hello there,

We are the Big Bad Brick Gang. You probably can't believe we struck here, but we did. You'll never figure out what makes us choose a place to strike. By the way, if you want to call us the BBBG, that's fine with us.

Yours truly,
The Big Bad Brick Gang,
aka the BBBG

"We'll never figure out what makes them choose a place to strike," Mimi said. "What in the world do Boards and Swords have in common?"

"Nothing," Stew said.

"That's right, son," Harvey said proudly. "You're a genius."

"They rhyme," I said.

Mimi frowned. "What rhymes?"

"The names of the stores," I said, and turned to Muriel Distinguished. "Are there any other stores with similar-sounding names?"

"There's an electrical supply store, Cords, just down the street," the shopkeeper said, "and across the square is Gourds, where I buy all my decorative squashes. There used to be a Scandinavian travel place called Fjords, but it went out of business last winter."

I turned to the Mitchums. "The crimes of the Big Bad Brick Gang appear to be following a pattern. If you like, I'd be happy to help you keep an eye on those two other businesses."

"First of all, let's call them the BBBG,"

Harvey said. "And thirdly, we don't need your help when we have Stewart around. Our son is smarter than you, and more handsome. Isn't that right, Stewie?"

"You're so nice to me, Daddy," Stew said, and when his father chuckled and turned his back, he gave me a big, hard poke.

That was Saturday.

•

I asked the Bellerophon brothers, known as Pip and Squeak, to drive me around the old neighborhood as soon as the sun came up. All was quiet at Cords. Nothing was amiss at Gourds. But then through the taxi window I saw more shattered glass, and the Bellerophons deposited me in front of another vandalized business with a stunned shopkeeper and police officers arguing in front of it. There were pink and red petals on the sidewalk, along with the familiar sight of broken glass, and painted petals decorated the sign over the door. I looked at the name of the business and sighed the sigh of someone who's wrong and sighs about it.

"And I'm telling you, Harvey," Mimi said, "the dead bird is what changed her mind about her mother's old suitor, and that's why she came back."

"I don't know why you bother to read at all," Harvey said, "when you understand no more than a garden slug."

"I'll slug you if you keep talking like that," Mimi growled.

"I can't believe you said that! Apologize at once!"

"You're the one who got me angry enough to say it! Apologize for provoking me!"

"Apologize for provoking *me*!"

"Apologize for provoking my provocation!"

My shoes crackled on a piece of broken glass, and the bickering Mitchums turned to glare at me. "You have some nerve coming around here," Harvey said. "Boards and Swords don't rhyme with the name of this store. It's not even half-rhyme!"

"Chrysanthemums," Mimi said, "is a Respectable family business, and we are helpless to bring the BBBG to justice." She waved another piece of paper, but I didn't need to read it. I was sure it said that the police were helpless to bring the gang to justice.

"I'm Lemony Snicket," I said to the shopkeeper. "I'm sorry about what happened to your store. I had a theory about what was going on, and I'm sad to say I was wrong about it. I assume you're Ms. Respectable?"

The shopkeeper gave me a curious look. "My name is Smith," she said. "Delphinium Smith. Our family happens to be respectable, but it's not our name."

"I'm sorry," I said, although I was used to asking the wrong questions during my days in

Stain'd-by-the-Sea. "Was anything stolen, Ms. Smith?"

"My daughter's just checking," the shop-keeper said. "The brick almost hit the bed where she slept last night." She dropped her broom for a moment and cupped both hands to her mouth to call into the shop. "Florence!"

A girl emerged from the shop, giving her mother an apologetic look and holding a book I recognized. "Sorry, Mother. I got distracted by a good part of my book. Peter is just escaping from Barbados and has decided to be a buccaneer."

"It's about to get even better," I said.

"Don't tell me what happens next," Florence said. "I hate having a book spoiled."

"I would never do such a thing," I said.

"Another bookworm," the shopkeeper said to me with a grimace. "I don't know where Florence gets those books. Personally, I think literature is garbage. None of my daughters are allowed a library card, and Florence can't have a bookshelf in her room unless she builds it herself."

"I'm sorry to hear you say that," I said. "It makes me less enthusiastic about telling you I've solved the crimes. But perhaps the guilty parties will work together to repair the windows and explain their behavior."

"Hold on," Harvey Mitchum said. "Are you saying you know how to stop the Big Bad Brick Gang? Because according to something I read recently, no one will ever figure out how to stop them."

"They're not really a gang," I said. "Just two people in cahoots."

"Name them," Mimi said, "so we can arrest the cahooters."

"Yes," Harvey said, for once in agreement with his wife. "We can't have any cahooting in this town."

I didn't tell them. Nor did I tell Theodora anything that evening, when she came home and asked me what I'd done all weekend. I told her nothing and she gave me a teacup decorated with an ugly pattern. Unchaperoned people often do things that respectable adults don't understand, and the unchaperoned people like to keep it that way. The gang probably wouldn't strike again, I thought, putting my teacup on the floor where I might carelessly step on it in the morning.

And that was Sunday.

• • •

The conclusion to "Bad Gang" is filed under "Homemade Furniture," page 225.

SILVER SPOON.

I was in my favorite seat in the library, but it wasn't helping me like the book any better. It was a book people kept putting in my hands and telling me I was going to love, the way the doctor tells you the needle won't hurt a bit. The book began the way it always began before I gave up on it: with a man carrying around a drawing of a snake that had just eaten, and asking people what they thought of it. I thought it was no way to start up a conversation.

"I hate to interrupt," Dashiell Qwerty said to me, which is a better way.

"It's quite all right," I said to Stain'd-by-the-Sea's only librarian.

"I thought you wouldn't mind," Qwerty said. "You were scowling pretty hard at that book."

"Everyone else seems to like it, so I thought I'd give it another try."

"Perhaps I can suggest a better way to occupy your time."

"I'm still not sure I'm ready for that book about the woman who falls asleep and kills a horse."

"That's not what I was suggesting. Some library patrons need some assistance, and I thought you might be able to help."

"Why me?"

"Because I understand you're good at assisting people," Qwerty said, "and because it's closing time and you might not have anything better to do."

I looked out through one of the library's

drafty windows. I hadn't noticed it was so late. The sky was dark blue twilight, pretty to look at but lonely to walk under. Qwerty was right. I didn't have anything better to do. I put the book back on the shelf and waited for Qwerty to turn off the lights and give the room one last look before he locked up and I followed him out into the quiet streets of town. We walked across the scraggly lawn, where the ruins of an old statue lay sad and cold in the evening air. Qwerty rattled his fingers against it as we walked by. The librarian was the sort of librarian who didn't look like a librarian. His hair was an unusual kind of unusual—a ragged, angular mess that he must have thought was stylish—and he always wore a leather jacket with bits of metal stuck here and there. But he was very much a librarian like other librarians, because I knew I could trust him. Even so I paused for a moment when, after several silent blocks, he stopped at a large, gaping hole in a chain-link fence. Behind the fence

I could see some unhealthy-looking shrubs, peppered with litter and pressed up against the fence as though trying to escape.

"Where are we going?" I asked.

"I told you," Qwerty said. "Some of my patrons need help."

"And they live *here*?"

"At present they live in a small camp on the outskirts of town."

"At present?"

"That means 'right now.' "

"I know what it means. Where do they live the rest of the time?"

"Wherever they can find shelter," Qwerty said. "They're a group of people who move from town to town."

"So they're not citizens of Stain'd-by-the-Sea," I said.

"They're visitors, and readers," Qwerty said, "like you."

He stepped through the fence and I followed.

The wind picked up paper bags and old candy wrappers and whirled them around my legs as we walked through the rustling landscape. Qwerty was right. I was a visitor in town. I did not know how long I would stay, and each day seemed to uncover another mysterious event in a town full of them. Stain'd-by-the-Sea was the sort of place where secrets lurked everywhere, like shuddering plants behind a fence I'd never thought twice about. Qwerty was also right about my being a reader, and I'd read here and there about people who lived as Qwerty had described. Drifters, some people called them. There were other words, too.

The sun left the sky slowly, leaving pale, hovering streaks above us, and before long we were at a small grove of trees that looked shady. "Shady" is a word which means "giving shade." It is also a word which means "ever so slightly sinister." I followed Qwerty into the grove, stepping over roots and ducking under branches that stretched out like spooky handshakes.

At last we reached the drifters' camp, which was little more than a few tents pitched on dirt that had been tramped flat. There was a small circle of stones where a fire cast its warm red glow onto the faces of perhaps ten people, huddled in blankets together around the flames. They were mostly men, looking tired and dirty, although there were at least two women, and I could see a dog lying close to the fire with one eye open and one ear missing.

"Qwerty," said the man with the longest beard. "Welcome. Do you want soup? Who's your companion?"

"This is Lemony Snicket," Qwerty said, "and soup would be nice."

"Nice to know you, Snicket," said the bearded man. "Have a seat. Are you going to read to us, Qwerty?"

"I hope so," said one of the women, whose voice was hoarse or perhaps just exhausted. "Last

night you stopped at the part where the book-case fell on him."

"Last night," Qwerty said, sitting on a log and motioning me to join him, "you were telling me about some trouble that Randall got himself into."

"He didn't get himself in trouble," said the woman. "Trouble came and found him, and it arrived by limousine."

"Let Randall tell the story," the bearded man said, and the drifters turned their eyes to a short, meek figure who sat on the ground next to the dog. He was a man a little younger and a little cleaner than the others, wearing a pair of glasses that were slightly askew, a word which here means "crooked, and should be repaired." He looked at us nervously and patted the dog with one gloved hand.

"That's a handsome dog, Randall," Qwerty said gently.

Randall smiled. "He's not handsome," he

said, "but he's my best friend in the world and one of the dearest things in my life."

"What's his name?" I asked. "And what's the trouble?"

"His name is Ashbery," Randall said, "and the trouble is that one of my other dearest things was stolen from me."

"What was stolen?" I asked, thinking of all the things that had gone missing in Stain'd-by-the-Sea. It was as if the entire town were sinking into quicksand, item by item, never to be seen again.

"A silver spoon," Randall said, "engraved with the letter *R*. It was a gift from my grandfather when I was born." He sighed and looked at the crackling fire for a moment. "I've lost everything else from my old life, but I've managed to hold on to my grandfather's gift. Until yesterday."

"What happened yesterday?"

"Smogface Wiley stole his spoon is what

happened," said one of the drifters. "He's a low-down scoundrel in high-priced clothing."

"The Wileys," Qwerty explained to me, "are a wealthy family who own businesses all over the area, from lumber to tube socks. Smogface is the only Wiley left in town. Smogface isn't his given name, as you might have guessed, but it's what everyone calls him because of his habit of smoking cigarillos."

"They smell terrible," the bearded drifter said, "but something tells me that man would smell terrible anyway."

The drifters muttered in agreement, and Randall patted Ashbery glumly. "Wiley drove past me a few days ago," he continued, "and saw me using the spoon to eat a can of peaches in light syrup."

"Were you here at the camp?" I asked.

"No," Randall said. "I was working in town. I'm a poet by trade, but lately I've done a lot of window washing. Diceys Department Store had me wash their windows for a few coins and some canned goods they had lying around. Ashbery stayed behind to guard the camp as usual. Nobody hires a window washer who brings his dog around."

"Same with lizards," said another man by the fire.

"Smogface had his driver stop and rolled down the limousine window to ask me about the spoon. He wanted it for himself and kept offering me things. He offered a carton of cigarillos, but I don't smoke. He offered me his pinkie ring, but I have no use for one. He offered me a ride in his limousine and a hot bath at his mansion. I was tempted, but I still had windows to wash."

"Why did he want the spoon so much?" I asked.

"He said he had a collection," Randall said, "but I think he just wanted to see me eat canned peaches with my hands."

The bearded man shook his head in disgust

and handed Qwerty and me each a steaming mug of soup. The mugs had the name of a hardware store I'd never heard of, along with an image of an octopus holding a bunch of tools. The store was gone now, probably. The soup was very hot and very thin, more like earthy tea than soup. I didn't like sipping it, so I asked another question.

"What happened yesterday?" I said.

"Yesterday we all went to harvest mushrooms out by Blotted Boulevard," Randall said. "Armadale over there is good at spotting the edible ones. When we returned to camp after sundown, Ashbery was barking like crazy, the spoon was gone, and there was an extinguished cigarillo smoking by the fire."

"Did you ask Wiley about it?"

"Of course I did," Randall said. "I went right to his mansion last night."

"We all wanted to go with him," said the woman, "but Randall insisted on going alone."

"The mansion is that big building over on Nib Court, with a big brass walrus out front. It's a nice enough place, but nobody was nice to me there. Wiley wouldn't even see me. He had some servant throw me out on my ear. Qwerty told me he knew someone who'd retrieved a stolen object from the Sallis mansion. He thought you could help me, too."

To be polite, I took a sip of soup and tried to think about the Sallis mansion instead of the earthy taste in my mouth. There was a much bigger case I was working on, a more complicated one that involved the enormous house the Sallis family had once occupied, along with a butler and numerous other servants. "I'll go out there tomorrow morning," I said, "and see what I can do."

"I'd be most grateful," Randall said. "Anytime you need a sonnet, I'm your man."

I thanked him and stood up and headed out of the grove with Qwerty. We were quiet all the way back to the Lost Arms, and later that night, when I got into my bed in the Far East Suite, the narrow bed and the dusty room felt much more comfortable than usual as I thought about Randall and the spoon and all the people huddled around the fire. Drifters. Tramps. Vagabonds. Derelicts. So many words for such people, and all of them unflattering.

The next day I made my way to the Wiley mansion. It was a bright, quiet morning, and the last of Stain'd-by-the-Sea's birds fought over a few worms wriggling on the sidewalk. I found the house easily enough. A brass walrus stands out. The driveway was paved with seashells and occupied mostly by a long, black limousine. It was a handsome enough car, but the windows needed washing. In a storybook, the villain lives in a castle and the hero lives in the woods. I had to remind myself that this wasn't a storybook. The meek, bespectacled drifter could be the villain, I thought, making up a story about Smogface

Wiley just because he has a fancy house and gets driven around in a limousine.

A servant answered the doorbell and just stood there glaring at me, waiting for me to state my business. I stated my name instead and told her I was visiting from the city. She shut the door again. Birds chirped. She came back and let me in.

Smogface Wiley was seated at the end of a very long, very polished wood table, as if he had invited a bunch of people to a fancy breakfast and they had all forgotten to come. There were folded napkins and monogrammed silverware at each place setting but food at only one. Wiley looked about halfway through his breakfast. There was a plate with a half-eaten fried egg and a small pile of roasted potatoes where a large one would have fit. There was a bowl half full of cereal and a basket with half a blueberry muffin. Wiley had a fresh peach in front of him and in his mouth a cigarillo, which is a bit like a cigar and a bit like a cigarette and more than a bit like a smelly nuisance. The smoke from the cigarillo made a small cloud that had for some reason stuck around his nose. "Smokynose" would have been a better nickname, I thought.

"Good morning, Mr. Wiley."

"Good morning," Wiley replied, and picked up a knife and fork emblazoned with fancy *W*s. "Had I known you were coming, I would have had breakfast prepared for you. Unfortunately, there's only enough for me."

"That is unfortunate," I said as Wiley began to cut the peach in half.

"It's a delight to have a visitor from the city," Wiley said. "Stain'd-by-the-Sea has fewer and fewer well-bred people like ourselves." His fork clattered on the plate, and the peach rolled around a little in the struggle. "Well-bred" is a word which doesn't mean anything at all, but which some people use to make themselves feel better than others. I watched Wiley fight with the peach and thought of myself as "well-bred" and him as something else.

"Perhaps you'd like to join me for dinner tonight," Wiley said. "My friend Mr. Samsa has taken ill, so you could take his place. I personalize the menu and decorations for each of my guests. It's a very well-bred gathering."

"I'm sure it is," I told him, and looked down the long table. "You're certainly entertaining a large number of guests."

"Twenty-five," Wiley said with satisfaction. "Until recently I couldn't have that many."

"Why is that?"

Wiley spooned a bite of peach into his mouth with a well-bred spoon. "I'm sure you didn't come here to hear about my social life," he said.

"That is true," I admitted. "I'm looking for a lost spoon."

Wiley gestured down the table. "These are mine."

"The one I'm looking for isn't," I said. "It

belongs to a man named Randall whom I believe you met a few days ago outside Diceys Department Store."

"That's right," Wiley said. "I was out shopping for ascots and asked him to move aside so I could admire my reflection in the window."

"Did he?"

"Did he what?"

"Did he move aside?"

"He did."

"Did you notice he was eating with a spoon?"

"I noticed he was eating," Wiley said, eating. "He was getting light syrup all over himself."

"Have you seen him since?"

"I have not," Wiley said, with a waggle of his smoky head. "My sort of people don't associate with greasy drifters and one-eared dogs. I spend my time entertaining an assortment of well-bred friends."

"You had another dinner party last night?"

"Yes."

"Can you prove it?"

Wiley swallowed his bite of peach and then blew a smoke ring toward my face. "Of course," he said. "Ask Dr. Auchincloss. Ask Madame Blavatsky. Ask any of the twenty-two other people on my guest list."

"If I ask them, will they say you were here all night entertaining them?"

Wiley's eyes flashed above the cloud of smoke. "If you ask them, they will ask you why you're asking."

"Perhaps it's because I admire your ascot," I said.

"I'm beginning to think you're not well-bred at all," Wiley said. "I bet you don't even know what an ascot is."

"An ascot," I said, "is a fancy scarf. And you are a liar. Give it back this instant."

"You can't talk to me like that," Wiley said, rising from the table. "I'll have you thrown out on your ear."

"You should stop saying that, Smogface," I told him. "It's your mistake. Now get me the stolen spoon or I'll tell all your guests how you acquire your personalized decorations."

•   •   •

The conclusion to "Silver Spoon" is filed under "Twenty-Five Guests," page 229.

VIOLENT BUTCHER.

It seemed as good a day as any to go to Black Cat Coffee, one of Stain'd-by-the-Sea's last businesses and certainly its most unusual one. There was a girl who spent a lot of time there, drinking the strong, bitter coffee served up by the place's enormous and elaborate machinery. The girl was Ellington Feint, and she's a long story all by herself. I hadn't seen her in quite some time, and I thought Black Cat Coffee was my best chance of spotting her. But as soon as I hit the corner of Caravan and Parfait, I knew I'd walked into a different story altogether. My path was largely blocked by a large man sitting largely on the curb. He was reading a magazine and wearing an apron, although he was such a big man that it looked like he was reading a matchbook and wearing a hand-kerchief. Normally, I don't like to use the word "mountainous" about a person, but this man was so large, and his shoulders so peaked, and his beard so rough and scraggly like a grouping of trees on his chin, that he actually looked like a mountain. I didn't have the proper equipment to climb him, so I tried a different approach.

"Excuse me," I said, but the man shook his mountainous head.

"Sorry, chief," the man said. "I can't let anybody in here. You shouldn't drink coffee, anyway. It's bad for you."

"It's bad for you if you never do anything bad for you," I said, "but I'm not here for coffee. I'm looking for someone."

"Well, I'm looking for someone, too," the man said, "and until I find who I'm looking for, I can't let you in."

"Maybe I can help you," I said. "I've been known to find a person or two. It's more or less my job."

"My job's being a butcher," the man said. He pointed to his apron, which I now saw was quite stained, and held up his magazine, which I now saw was called *Read Meat*. "My name's Mack. I used to work over at Partial Foods, but now I'm freelancing. I don't know you. Usually I don't like people I don't know, so why don't you ske-daddle? I can't let anyone in here until I find the kid I'm here to find."

"Maybe we're looking for the same person," I said.

He looked interested, but not mountain-ously so.

"Maybe," he said.

"Mine is a girl," I said. "A little taller than

I am, with black hair, green eyes, and unusual eyebrows."

"Wrong," the man said, with another gigantic shake of his head. "Mine's a boy named Drumstick, and he's preternaturally short, with curly red hair and extremely normal eyebrows. I don't know what color his eyes are, because I never noticed. He's my son and I need to find him."

"Preternaturally" is a word which here means "extra." I was beginning to preternaturally dislike this butcher. "What makes you think your son is at Black Cat Coffee?"

"Because I saw him run right in there."

"Why did he do that?"

"For the reason that I was chasing him."

"Why were you chasing him?"

"For the reason that I would hit him with this magazine," Mack said. "Drumstick was a very bad boy today. I told him to stick around the house and not go outside, and then he kept getting in my way and wouldn't leave. I yelled at him about it for around an hour, and then he told me he was going to take the train into the city to live with his mother. She's a butcher, too, but not as good with venison. He took all the money he's earned repairing women's shoes and ran out the door. I chased him here."

"Why did you stop at the door?" I asked, hoping the answer was "Because I realized I was doing something wrong."

"I got real tired," the man said instead. "Now I'm just going to wait him out. He can't stay in there forever."

"I don't see why not," I said. "There's bread and coffee, and a piano that plays lonely tunes all by itself."

"Say, I have an idea," Mack said, leaning in close to talk quietly. His breath was warm and full of meat. "Why don't you go in with me? If I go in alone, I know he'll slip away. He moves quick as a game hen. But two of us could corner him. If you help me out here, I'll give you a rack of lamb."

"No, thanks," I said, thinking that it wasn't a good day to go to Black Cat Coffee after all. It was a good day to sit at the library by myself and fill my head with something other than the story of this family.

"Nothing I can say to convince you?" Mack asked.

"I'm afraid not."

"You ever get hit with a magazine?" Mack asked me. His voice was friendly enough, but he was rolling *Read Meat* up into a mean-looking tube. "They say it stings something awful."

I looked up and down the empty streets. "Well," I said, "you've convinced me."

"Thattaboy," Mack said, and rose up from the sidewalk like a new volcanic island. He lurched through the door with thattaboy following glumly behind. Black Cat Coffee looked the same as always and as empty as usual, but

even when the place was empty, it was usually loud. The vast, rackety machinery which produced Black Cat Coffee's only refreshments was completely still, and the piano which usually played melancholy tunes was closed and quiet. It was quiet enough that I stopped to listen for a moment. Then I walked up to the counter and looked at the three buttons the place had instead of people who worked there. If you pressed the *C* button, the shiny machinery behind the counter whirred into life and brewed a single cup of coffee. The *B* button produced a small loaf of hot, fresh bread, which I liked much better. The *A* button activated a folding staircase which clicked into place so you could walk up to the attic, which was a good place to hide secrets. If I were Drumstick, I thought, I'd hide in the attic. I would also change my name.

"I thought I heard a crash after my son ran in here," Mack said, and headed over to peer behind the counter, and I peered with him. There were cups and saucers stacked up on shelves, and a surprising mess on the floor. Someone had over-turned a dented metal trash can, which lay on its side surrounded by bread crusts, glass bottles, a cracked flowerpot, and what looked like a flat-tened clump of tissue paper. But there wasn't a preternaturally small boy with curly hair and eyes his father should have looked at. If you look someone in the eyes, really look at them, you are much less likely to hit them. You are less likely to even think of it.

"I saw a movie once where something impor-tant was hidden in a piano," I said.

"I saw that one," Mack said. "All those fools singing in French. Hold on and I'll check."

I held on and he checked. Drumstick was not inside the piano. I didn't think he would be. A piano that plays by itself is called a player piano, and it has various mechanisms inside it that would prevent even the smallest person from crawling inside. I did not want Mack to find his son, but the trouble is that not wanting someone to be found is almost the same as wanting to find them. In either case, you need to know where they are.

"There is another door to Black Cat Coffee," I said hopefully. "Maybe Drumstick simply ran back out again."

Mack either grunted or laughed. It's hard to tell which with some people. He walked to the door I'd pointed out, his thick feet moving on the floor like sad toads. It was closed, and it was still closed when Mack was through rattling and pounding it. "Locked," he said. "Locked tight as last year's pants. Drumstick didn't leave. My son is hidden somewhere in here. I'd bet my juiciest veal chops on it."

I looked again at the machinery and looked again at the piano. I looked everywhere in the quiet room but at the button marked *A*. I did not like Mack, but I could not disagree with his reasoning. He wiped his hands on his apron and walked slowly toward the counter. *"Drumstick!"* he called. "Come on out and get your punishment! I'm going to wallop you over and over, and then we'll go home and have some bone marrow for supper!"

"Bone marrow?" I said, trying my best to stand in his way. "What's the best way to prepare that, in your opinion? Roasted? Creamed? Discarded?"

Mack glared at me and looked over my shoulder. "I forgot about that staircase," he said, and reached over me to press the *A* button. The staircase whirred into life and descended with great creakings and groanings. "That's why he threw all that trash around," the butcher said, raising his voice over the noise. "To cover up for this sound. Then he ran up and hid in the attic. Well, he's caught now, like a cow on my workbench." He waved his magazine back and forth for practice and began to thump up the stairs. I moved, too. By the time he was up the stairs, I was behind the counter. I waited and I kept waiting. I was listening closely, but it was hard to listen closely while Mack kept calling "Drumstick!" in a fake friendly voice that made me shudder. Then Mack was all the way up the stairs and then I heard it, a small metallic sound that made me press the button, the one marked *A*. There were more metallic sounds as the staircase folded itself up again and Mack started yelling. The button in the attic was tricky to find, so it would take a little while for Mack to lower the staircase and get down again. I hoped it was enough to give a head start to a preternaturally small boy with curly hair, normal eyebrows, and hazel eyes, fleeing toward safety and his mother.

• • •

The conclusion to "Violent Butcher" is filed under "Small Sound," page 233.

TWELVE OR THIRTEEN.

"Lemony Snicket," said Moxie Mallahan. She was talking to me. "Do you want to see something funny?"

It was an ordinary day, and Moxie had found me sitting on the lawn in front of one of Stain'd-by-the-Sea's most impressive buildings, looking at a large object. The building had once been City Hall and was now a library in one half and a police station in the other. The lawn had once been pretty but was now scraggly, and the large object I was looking at had once been an enormous statue and was now a metal lump, following a suspicious explosion some years previous. The explosion and the lump were part of my biggest case, and on some ordinary days I liked to sit and look at the statue's remains, hoping that a new clue would drop upon me. So far the only thing to drop upon me had been an acorn. An acorn was not a clue to anything, as far as I could tell. Something funny seemed like it could be a nice break.

"What kind of funny?" I asked her. "Funny like a clown onstage? Or funny like a clown hanging around the entrance to a bank?"

"The bank one." Moxie sat down next to me and opened her typewriter case with a click.

"What's the news, Moxie?"

"I was in the archives of *The Stain'd Lighthouse*," she told me, "looking through the articles my mother wrote when she was still a reporter in town."

"I bet she was a good one," I said, "if her daughter is any indication."

"I like to think I developed some of my journalism skills on my own," Moxie said.

"I'm sure she'll be very proud when she sees you again."

She handed me an envelope. "In the meantime, take a look."

"I don't see anything funny about an envelope," I said.

Moxie took off her hat and rolled her eyes. "And I don't see anything funny about that remark," she said. "Why don't you look *inside* the envelope?"

"Good idea," I said, but when I slid the crumpled newspaper article into my hands, I still didn't see anything funny.

"*Tepid Turnout for Frome Race*," I read out loud. "*Only a dozen sledders competed in this year's race down Homily Hill for the Ethan Frome Festival. Organizers said attendance at the auction was also a disappointment, despite such distinguished items as an oil painting of Gary Dorian, Stain'd-by-the-Sea's famed cosmetician. Hot cider sales were also low. Complete story on page thirty-four."*

There wasn't any more to it, so I turned my eyes to Moxie and shrugged.

"Don't shrug at me, Snicket."

"I shrug when there's something to shrug about," I explained. "I'm sorry it's not a very interesting article, but it's not your mother's fault. It sounds like the Ethan Frome Festival wasn't very interesting."

"You're wrong there," Moxie said, her voice a little wistful. "The Ethan Frome Festival was once a wondrous event in Stain'd-by-the-Sea. Every winter there would be a large auction where people would bid large sums of money on various items, and all the money would be donated to the library. After the auction there would be a competitive sled race down to the bottom of the hill, where the fastest sledder would win a medal and a very handsome fountain pen provided by Ink Inc. But when the ink industry began to fade, the festival got smaller and smaller until they canceled it altogether."

"That's a sad story," I said, "but I don't see much funny about it."

"Take another look."

"*Tepid Turnout*—"

"Another *look*, Snicket. Not another read."

My eye moved to the photograph which accompanied the article. It wasn't a very good photograph, and it was made worse by the fading, shriveled paper on which it was printed.

"Looks like tough sledding," I said. "Lots of trees and rocks, unless those are just ink smudges."

"*The Stain'd Lighthouse* never smudged," Moxie said sternly, "and it's not the landscape I noticed. It's the sledders."

"This photograph was taken from the top

of Homily Hill," I said. "The sledders look like little bugs in the snow."

"How many bugs?"

I looked at the photograph again and then I looked at it again and once more. Then I looked at Moxie.

"I knew you'd catch on eventually," she told me.

"I count thirteen."

"So do I," Moxie said, taking the newspaper, "and the article says *a dozen*."

"Well, somebody miscounted."

"My mother was a very good journalist," Moxie said. "If she said there were a dozen sledders competing in the race, that's how many there were."

It is useless to argue with somebody about their mother. Even if you win the argument, you feel like a scoundrel. "Well, then perhaps someone just happened to be sledding down the same hill," I said. "Someone who wasn't competing."

"That doesn't seem very likely. If you liked sledding, why wouldn't you participate in the race?"

"I don't know why anyone likes sledding in the first place," I said. "Life goes downhill enough without speeding the process along. Was there a referee, perhaps?"

"There was no referee."

"Another photographer, then? Getting pictures of the racers close up?"

"At the time this article appeared, *The Stain'd Lighthouse* had only one photographer."

"A rock that happened to be shaped like a sledder?"

Moxie gave this last guess of mine the glare it deserved. "I was hoping a pair of fresh eyes would solve this mystery," she said. "I've been staring at this photograph for quite some time trying to figure it out."

"Fresh eyes might not be enough for figuring," I said. "We need more to go on than an old photograph. The rest of the article would be helpful. Where's page thirty-four?"

Moxie shook her head. "I searched the archives for hours, but page thirty-four is nowhere to be found."

"Do you mind if I ask you why you're investigating this particular mystery?" I said, looking back at the ruined statue. "I don't have to remind you that we have quite a bit of pressing business to attend to."

"Of course you don't have to remind me, Snicket," Moxie said. "I was investigating our big case, but I got distracted by this other crime."

"I don't know if you can call a mysterious photograph of sledders a crime," I said. "It's more like a curiosity."

"Well, I got curious about a theft that was committed on the day of the festival," Moxie said, "and I thought the photograph might be a clue."

"Theft?" I asked. "What was stolen?"

"An oil painting of Stain'd-by-the-Sea's famed cosmetician," Moxie said.

"Gary Dorian," I said. "That portrait was one of the auction's most distinguished items."

"I already know you read the article about the festival," Moxie said with a smile, opening her typewriter case again, "but there was an article about the theft in the next day's edition." She produced another envelope, and the envelope produced another scrap of newsprint. "The painting disappeared during the sled race but was found late that night in the home of Chase B. Willow."

"Who's Chase B. Willow?"

"He worked for Ink Inc. as a needle operator in the inkwells, needling ink out of the octopi."

I shivered a little. The giant needle machines extracting ink from the frightened octopi hiding down in deep wells were something that always made me uneasy, from the first time I saw the devices on my way into town. "Why would a needle operator steal a painting?"

"Mr. Willow always maintained his innocence," Moxie said, using a phrase which here means "said he didn't do it," and she looked down at the second article. "*'I'm a happily married man,' Mr. Willow told reporters as police led him out of his house. 'I have absolutely no interest in cosmeticians.' Despite these protests, Mr. Willow was arrested and charged with the theft of the painting, which the officers found in Mr. and Mrs. Willow's attic in what was described as 'more or less plain sight, leaning against an antique headboard.'*"

"Were the officers the Mitchums?" I asked, thinking of Stain'd-by-the-Sea's only police officers. "I'm surprised they found the painting. Frankly, I'm surprised they found the attic."

"It wasn't the Mitchums," Moxie said. "It says here it was the Officers Durham. Stain'd-by-the-Sea had a whole police squad back then."

"So the Durhams arrested Mr. Willow?"

"They did more than arrest him," Moxie

said. "They arrested him and put him on trial, and when he was found guilty, they shipped him off to prison in the city. He's still there."

"A prison term seems fair punishment for someone who stole a valuable painting."

"I agree," Moxie said, "but I don't think Mr. Willow committed the crime."

"Were the Durhams corrupt?"

"The Durhams were two of the bravest and most honest women in Stain'd-by-the-Sea. If they arrested Mr. Willow, they thought he was guilty."

"He must have looked pretty guilty if the painting was found in his attic," I said, "and his excuse about being married doesn't make much sense."

"His alibi doesn't make much sense either," Moxie said.

"Where did Mr. Willow say he was while the painting was stolen?" I asked.

"The whole town knew where he was,"

Moxie said. "He was winning a medal and a very handsome fountain pen. Chase B. Willow won the sled race at the Ethan Frome Festival that year. The police deduced that he stole the painting, sledded down the hill with it, and hid it in his attic. That night he had a party celebrating his victory, and invited several of his friends in the police force. During a game of hide-and-seek, they found the painting in the attic."

"What kind of thief," I asked, "invites police officers to his home where he has hidden a stolen item?"

"And what kind of thief," Moxie asked, "tries to win a sledding contest in the middle of a crime?"

"It would be difficult enough to hide a stolen painting on a sled going downhill," I agreed, "without everyone watching you win a medal and a fountain pen."

"Nevertheless, Mr. Willow was found guilty and sent to prison," Moxie said. "The portrait of Gary Dorian was auctioned off the following year, the festival continued to decline, and Willow's wife divorced her imprisoned husband and moved in with a lawn mower technician. The whole story was more or less forgotten until I stumbled upon it in the archives."

"What else about the crime is in those archives?" I asked.

"I'm putting together a file," Moxie said, "but it's taking a while. The *Lighthouse* archives are really in a shambles. There are articles and photographs everywhere."

"Photographs?" I said.

"Of course," Moxie said. "When you see a picture in a newspaper, it's just one of dozens the photographer has taken that day. The editors print their favorite one, and the rest are filed away."

"Let's go," I said.

"To the archives?"

"To the archives," I told her, and to the archives we went.

The archives of *The Stain'd Lighthouse* lived in a lighthouse that had once served as the newspaper office and a beacon for ships at sea and now just served as the Mallahan home. It was a bit of a walk from where Moxie had found me, and the journalist and I wound our way through the deserted streets of Stain'd-by-the-Sea and then up a curvy road that led to the lighthouse. We passed rows of uninhabited houses with broken windows and overgrown lawns, and I found myself wondering how much work a lawn mower technician would have in a town like Stain'd-by-the-Sea, which seemed to grow wilder and more untamed each day.

"You know where the archives are," Moxie said, gesturing to the spiral staircase as we stepped inside the lighthouse. "I'll meet you up there after I pour us some limeade and check on my father."

"Give him my regards," I said.

"I will if he's awake," she said, and ducked into the kitchen while I climbed up the stairs. I had visited the archives of *The Stain'd Lighthouse* before, and it was always a tiresome task. There were files and stacks of paper everyplace, sometimes very organized and sometimes not at all. If you opened the windows, the breeze tended to blow papers around and make your job worse, but if you kept them closed, the room was so stuffy you wanted to take a nap. I probably needed a nap but didn't want to take one, like almost everyone I knew.

There was a large, flat desk where Moxie had been working, and I sat there and looked through the papers she had assembled, until I found a sheaf of photographs taken during the Ethan Frome Festival three years previously. By the time Moxie came in with the limeade in tall, frosted glasses, I was frowning at a photo of a large, smiling man with a medal around his neck. He had a sled under one arm and was using his other hand to raise a fountain pen high up in the air in a victory salute. Around him was a crowd frozen in mid-applause, their breaths cloudy in the winter air.

"I'm guessing this is Mr. Willow," I said.

"Yes," she said, leafing through the photographs. "Here's another picture of him right before the race, with his wife holding his sled while he takes a sip of hot cider."

"I don't see his wife in the victory crowd," I said.

"Maybe she was preparing for the party. Look, here's another photograph of Mr. Willow, although you can only see his back."

"Then we can't be sure it's him," I said.

"It's the same sweater," Moxie said, "and his sledding number is pinned to it there, see? Number Four. It's printed on the sled, too."

"There's no number on the sled when his wife's holding it."

"It's right there, in the victory photo. See?"

I turned my eyes from Chase B. Willow taking a sip of cider to look again at Chase B. Willow winning the pen. He didn't look much like a criminal, but plenty of people grin after doing terrible things.

"Was the painting in a frame?" I asked.

"It was leaning against a headboard," Moxie reminded me. "So it was probably framed."

"I guess he could hide a framed painting under his sweater," I said, "but it doesn't seem likely. His shoulders would look square."

Moxie had found another picture, this one of a chalkboard someone had carried to the top of Homily Hill. The numbers one through fifty were chalked on it, but only twelve numbers had names after them. "Twelve sledders," she said, "and twelve sledders only. See for yourself."

I saw for myself:

1. Mrs. Williams
2. Dr. Carlos
3. Mr. Williams
4. Mr. Willow
5. Mrs. Summerover
6. Dr. River
7. Mr. Noleaf
8. Dr. Bitten
9. Mr. Crimson
10. Mrs. Cling
11. Mr. Paler
12. Mr. Loth

"Two people named Williams," I said.

"Yes, a married couple," Moxie said. "You've met them, Snicket. They work over at the distillery."

"I wonder if they found it difficult to compete against each other," I said.

"I wouldn't think so. They competed in the contest for years, when Mrs. Williams was still Miss Herman."

"Are there any other married couples on the list?"

"Dr. Carlos is married to Mr. Loth," Moxie said. "She kept her maiden name when she married him."

"Did Willow's wife do that?"

"I don't think so. My mother referred to her as Mrs. Willow in the article."

"Do you know what she did for a living? Was she a doctor?"

"She was a locksmith," Moxie said with

a frown. "What does that have to do with anything?"

"It has to do with getting an innocent man out of jail," I said. "The portrait of Gary Dorian may have been framed, but Chase B. Willow definitely was."

•   •   •

The conclusion to "Twelve or Thirteen" is filed under "Chalked Name," page 237.

MIDNIGHT DEMON.

"Thank you for coming, Mr. Snicket," said the old woman who answered the door. I need hardly describe her. I had been summoned, in a handwritten note on frilly stationery, to come to a rocking chair store, the only one in Stain'd-by-the-Sea. The place was called Cozy's, and in the window were three cozy rocking chairs gathered together in a cozy circle along with a cozy, furry dog asleep in a cozy basket, and the old woman who ran the place looked exactly like the sort of old woman who would ask you in a handwritten note on frilly stationery to come to her rocking chair store called Cozy's because she had something on her mind that worried her very much. If you're still having trouble picturing her, it might help to know that her name was Thomasina Cozy.

"Of course, Mrs. Cozy," I said. "This is a very lovely shop you have here."

She ushered me in and gestured around her at all the rocking chairs. "I'm afraid it's a shadow of its former self," she said, using a phrase which here means "not as good as it used to be." "In Stain'd-by-the-Sea's glory days, our rocking chairs were the prized possession of anyone who liked to sit. Nowadays we have hardly any customers, and those who wander in seem to prefer *stationary chairs*."

The old woman said "stationary chairs" as if it were the name of her worst enemy, and offered me a rocking chair to sit in. I took a seat and moved back and forth without wanting to. I preferred stationary chairs myself. I like chairs and I don't mind rocking, but when the two are combined it's seasickness to me. "Sometimes I think we should sell something else," Mrs. Cozy said, "but what else could be sold at a store called Cozy's?"

"Blankets," said a voice from the back of the shop. It sounded like a young man.

"Pillows." The second voice sounded the same age, but female, and soon the voices were bouncing words back and forth, like a tennis match but much cozier.

"Pajamas."

"Teapots."

"Candles."

"Bubble bath."

"Photographs of kittens."

"Soft lighting."

"Loveseats."

"Sofas."

"Ottomans."

"Stationary chairs."

At this Mrs. Cozy clapped her hands and cried "Enough, twins!" and the owners of the voices stepped forward from behind a particularly tall rocking chair.

"These are the twins," the old woman said to me, and sure enough, the young man and the young woman looked quite a bit alike. The woman's hair was long and bushy, and the man's short and trim, but they had the same facial features, heights, and eyeglasses, and their hands felt identical as they shook mine and gave me their names.

"Tatiana," said the young woman.

"Treacle," said the young man.

"The twins are all I have since their father died in a stationary chair accident," Mrs. Cozy said.

"Our father died choking on a fish bone," Tatiana explained to me. "He just happened to be sitting at the time."

"I'm very sorry to hear it," I said.

Mrs. Cozy shook her head and made a noise I've never liked. "Tut tut" is what it was, and she rocked indignantly in her own chair. "Stationary chairs are the devil's handiwork. If human beings were meant to sit without moving back and forth, we wouldn't have leg muscles or wind."

"Mother," Treacle said patiently, "some people *like* stationary chairs. If we made a few changes to Cozy's, we could run a successful business, even in Stain'd-by-the-Sea, and we wouldn't have to live in that cramped apartment above the store."

"Tut tut," tutted Mrs. Cozy again. "I've taken care of that. Once Tatiana marries Baron von Pendle, all our problems will be solved."

"She doesn't want to marry him," Treacle said.

"He's a nice enough man," Tatiana said, "but we don't have much in common."

"You don't need much in common to have a

successful marriage," Mrs. Cozy said. "All your father and I had in common was that we both liked scary movies and eating big-boned fish. Baron von Pendle is a very wealthy man. His uncle invented the swing set, and when the two moving-seat families join together, I can go to my grave without worrying that you twins will end up living on the streets."

"You don't have to worry," Treacle said. "My sister and I are hard workers with a good education and sound business sense."

Tatiana nodded in agreement. "It's unlikely we'll end up living on the streets."

Mrs. Cozy turned to me. "Children think they know everything, don't you agree, Mr. Snicket?"

"Mother," Tatiana said, "Mr. Snicket *is* a child."

The shop owner squinted at me, and I wondered if she needed glasses, like her children. She didn't have them. "I hadn't heard you were a child," she said. "I'd heard you'd untangled a lot of problems in our little town, which is why I wrote to you."

My time in Stain'd-by-the-Sea had felt very entangling, rather than untangling, which simply means that I got into more trouble than I got out of, but there was something about the Cozy family that made me want to help them. Maybe it was the dog, still asleep in the window. People who owned a dog like this dog were likely to be kind people at heart. It was of a type so shaggy that you couldn't tell where its head was. Except for the dog's steady breathing, it looked more like a basket of hair than a pet. "I'm happy to be of service," I said.

Mrs. Cozy smiled and rocked steadily. "The marriage I've arranged for my daughter," she said, gesturing to Tatiana, "is being ruined by a demon."

I blinked at her and she rocked back at me. It's an important skill to know when not to say anything. It's not a skill that came naturally to me then, nor does it come naturally now, nor do I expect it to come naturally to me until I am dead, when I will be very, very good at it.

"I suppose you don't believe in demons," Mrs. Cozy said.

"I've never seen one," I said, "although I had a bad pediatrician for a few years."

"Baron von Pendle," Mrs. Cozy said, "has reported seeing my daughter walk along the Gobi Pier, which he can see from his front porch."

"That doesn't sound like a demon," I said.

"He sees her at midnight," she said. "Baron von Pendle has trouble sleeping, and so he often spends the night on his porch swing. He's spotted her for nine nights in a row. It has disturbed him greatly, and he told me he is reconsidering the marriage."

Mrs. Cozy gave me a meaningful look, but you should only give someone a meaningful look if they know what you are being meaningful about, and I had no idea. Walking on the Gobi Pier didn't seem like a good reason to reconsider marrying someone. I wasn't planning on marrying anytime soon, but I always assumed that my spouse would occasionally take walks. Mrs. Cozy must have sensed my confusion, because she stopped rocking, just for a moment, to explain to me what she meant. "There are words for a woman who walks the streets late at night," she said, with another meaningful look. "Words like insomniac."

"Insomniac?"

"It means someone who has trouble sleeping," Tatiana explained.

"I know what it means," I said, "but why should that bother the Baron?"

"Because he's an insomniac himself," Mrs. Cozy replied. "You can't have two insomniacs in the same household. Who will make the oatmeal? But that's not the point, Mr. Snicket. I tell you my daughter sleeps soundly. I know the Baron would never marry a sleepless woman, so I check each night before I go to sleep at nine fifteen, to make sure she is safe in bed. Yet somehow the Baron sees her roaming the pier at midnight. Something is taking the form of my daughter, to cancel the wedding and ruin my life. A demon is the only reasonable explanation."

Whether or not you believe in them, demons are not the only reasonable explanation for anything. By all accounts, demons are not reasonable at all. In fact, in some circumstances "reasonable" is a word which means "not a demon."

"Can you help us, Mr. Snicket?" Mrs. Cozy asked.

"I believe I can," I said, "but not until this evening. I'll come back about eleven o'clock."

"Return *here*?" Tatiana said. "But the demon is seen along the Gobi Pier, near the Baron's house."

I rose from my rocking chair, just when I

couldn't stand it any longer. "You and I," I told Tatiana, "will walk there together."

"Tut tut," Mrs. Cozy said.

"We'll stay out of the Baron's sight," I promised. "It's the only way to untangle this mess."

Mrs. Cozy frowned. "If you say so," she said.

"I say so," I said, and then I said so long. Just as I need hardly describe what Thomasina Cozy looked like, I probably don't have to tell you that I suspected Tatiana of sneaking out at night and walking along the pier herself. She didn't want to marry Baron von Pendle and probably thought this was the best way to cancel the wedding. But there are books all about how wrong I am. I spent the evening writing up a report of a case that doesn't concern you, and snuck out of the Lost Arms while my wild-haired chaperone slept. I hoped she was dreaming of buying a comb and that someday her dreams would come true.

The night was chilly and misty, what Mrs.

Cozy probably thought of as demon weather from all the scary movies she'd seen with her husband. I buttoned my coat and reminded myself always to be careful when eating fish.

Mrs. Cozy greeted me at the door in the sort of nightgown you would expect. Treacle was in some bright red pajamas, sitting in one of the rocking chairs in the window, reading a book and scratching either the head or the tail of the dog. Tatiana had on a long, dark coat and had her hair tucked neatly into a woolen cap. With her hair out of sight, she looked even more like her brother, although Treacle was not wearing lip gloss.

"Shall we?" she said.

"We shall," I replied, and Mrs. Cozy told me to be careful and that she would be up all night worrying and that she was going to bed. Tatiana and I walked down the cold and empty streets toward the area of town that once had piers at the edge of the sea. Now the sea was gone, drained away by Stain'd-by-the-Sea's ink industry, and the piers were just like long wooden fingers stretching toward nothing. It is a strange feeling to be walking around at night with a woman you hardly know, particularly if she is scheming against her mother. I didn't know what to say to her.

"It's cold this evening" is what I chose.

"It's all right, Mr. Snicket," she said. "You don't have to make small talk."

"Then let's talk about something important," I said. "Let's talk about your plan to trick your way out of marriage."

Tatiana frowned. "What do you mean?"

"I mean you know what I mean," I said. "You've been sneaking out at night and prowling along the Gobi Pier, in hopes that Baron von Pendle will cancel your wedding. Your romantic life is none of my affair, but I don't think it's right that you're tricking your mother."

"I'm not tricking her," Tatiana insisted. "I'm safe in bed every night, as my mother says."

"So you say," I said, "but we'll see what we'll see with you right where I can see you."

We'd reached the piers now, and in the darkness it looked like the sea might still be there, black and quiet in the night. I looked around me and spotted several houses with porches, although they were not close enough for me to see if they had swings, or sleepless barons. I motioned to Tatiana and we stood behind a deteriorating fishing shack.

"I don't see any demons," I said. "I wonder if that's because you're here with me?"

Tatiana sighed and took off her cap. "I don't know what the Baron has been seeing on the pier, but it's not me."

"Maybe the Baron is making the whole thing up."

"Why would he do that?"

"Maybe he's happy living as a bachelor, swinging on his porch."

"I don't think so. He seems quite eager to be my husband."

"Much more eager than you are."

"You're right that I don't want to marry him, but I was hoping to convince my mother to let my brother and me—"

Here the shopkeeper's daughter gasped and pointed a shaky finger at one of the empty piers. It wasn't empty now. There was a tall, slender figure, just out of the circle of dim light cast by a streetlamp. There were two circles where its face might have been—reflections of the streetlight in a pair of eyeglasses. It looked like it was wearing a long, black coat, or perhaps that was just more darkness, in a town with too much of it.

"That could be anyone," I said. "A boating enthusiast, for example."

The figure stepped closer to the streetlamp's dim glow.

"Anyone," I said, "with long hair like yours."

The figure took one step closer and turned its head slowly.

Tatiana screamed and ran away from the piers, her footsteps clattering on the cobblestones. I hurried after her as she gave out another cry, this one of pain, and I saw her crumple to the ground. I might have made a sound myself. Plenty of people make sounds when they are frightened. It's nothing to be ashamed of, and I don't have to describe the high-pitched wail of a sound I made if I don't want to.

When I reached Tatiana, she was in something of a heap and breathing heavily. I looked back at the pier to see if there was cause for any more screaming from either of us. The figure was gone.

"Are you all right?" I asked.

"Yes," she said. "I just tripped on my own panicked feet. How about you? I thought I heard you cry out."

"I think that was a nightingale," I said, helping us up.

"What was that we saw?"

"I'm not sure," I said.

"It looked like *me*," Tatiana said, looking at the empty pier. "It looked exactly like *me*. Do you really think it could be some kind of demon?"

"I don't know anything about demons," I said. "I don't know why a demon would want to look like the daughter of the owner of a rocking chair store, or why it would hang around on a pier that isn't a pier anymore. But I do know you have a twin brother with very similar facial features."

"He doesn't have long hair like mine," Tatiana said, "and he's at home reading."

"We can't be sure of that," I said. "We can't see him from here."

"Well, let's go home," Tatiana said. "I can wash the muck off my coat and make us some tea."

It was a quick if spooky walk back, and tea was already waiting for us at Cozy's. Treacle was there, in his red pajamas, with a steaming pot next to him on his rocking chair.

"I hope your demon hunt went better than my reading," he said. "This book was just spoiled by the arrival of Santa Claus."

"We also saw a mysterious nighttime figure," Tatiana said.

Treacle raised his eyebrows. "Oh?" he asked.

"Oh," I said, and knelt down on the ground. "What's your dog's name, by the way? I meant to ask you. Such a handsome specimen."

"We call her Tabby," said Treacle, "but her proper name is Tabitha."

"Come here, Tabitha," I said. "Come here, girl. Here, Tabitha. Here, dog."

The lump of fur looked around, and as she approached me, I finally saw which end was which. But it wasn't the only thing I saw. The twins gasped, but then looked at each other and then at me, with matching rueful smiles.

"You're very good liars," I said. "That might come in handy if you really want to sell people photographs of kittens. But wouldn't it be easier

147

just to tell your mother and the Baron that you don't want to get married?"

"Easier," Treacle said, "but not as much fun. Did you suspect?"

"Of course he suspected," Tatiana said, "but he didn't know for sure until you told him the name of the dog."

• • •

The conclusion to "Midnight Demon" is filed under "Panicked Feet," page 241.

THREE SUSPECTS.

Stain'd-by-the-Sea's only library, for as long as it lasted, was housed in the same building that held Stain'd-by-the-Sea's only police station. Whenever you went to one place, you had to look at the other. When I left the library I always saw the station door, and it never looked glad to see me. Literature and the law don't always get along. A great number of authors have been locked in prison for certain pieces of writing, and just as many police officers have been reduced to tears when reading a particularly powerful book. In Stain'd-by-the-Sea the only remaining police officers were a married couple known to most as the Officers Mitchum and known to me as no help at all. During all my investigations in this fading and endangered town, Harvey and Mimi Mitchum had been like a roller skate someone leaves in your way, so whenever I left the library I couldn't help glaring at the police station door as if it had sent me tumbling. This particular afternoon the door opened while I was glaring at it, and I found myself glaring at Harvey Mitchum, was who glaring right back at me.

"What do you want?" he asked me right away.

"Justice served and a root beer float," I said, "but I think I'll look elsewhere."

"I thought you were my son," Harvey said.

"That's very touching," I lied.

Harvey peeked over my shoulder. "I mean he was supposed to come help us."

"Is that the Snicket kid?" asked the voice of Mimi Mitchum from inside the station.

"Yes," Harvey said. "He was clomping out of the library like always."

"He's always snooping around," Mimi said. "Maybe he can snoop around this case."

"You think Snicket can help us?" Harvey called back to his wife in disbelief.

"It can't hurt to ask him while we wait for Stew," Mimi said.

"*You* ask him," Harvey said. He had turned all the way around, the better to snap at his wife, and for the first time in all my days in Stain'd-by-the-Sea, I had a close-up look at the back of Harvey Mitchum's head. If you would like to see what I saw, simply imagine a field of greasy, graying grass.

"You're right there," Mimi said. "I'm watching the suspects."

"I can watch them from here," Harvey said. "You come on over and talk to the kid."

"You do it."

"I don't want to."

"Don't be a baby, Harvey."

"Don't be an infant, Mimi."

"Don't be a fetus."

"Don't be a zygote."

"Don't be a woman and a man—"

I tapped Harvey Mitchum and the gray field turned around. "I couldn't help overhearing," I said. "I'm happy to be of assistance."

"You don't look happy," he said.

"I don't mean *cheerful*," I said. "I mean *willing*."

"*Willing* is more help than my husband," Mimi said from inside the station, and I maneuvered my way around Harvey's large, grumpy body into the station. It wasn't much more than a room with a couple of desks, a few file cabinets, and the smell of Mitchums, and in the back was a small cell that held prisoners until the train came from the city to transport them to trial. The cell was damp and cramped and couldn't hold very many people, and right then it held three men with grim mouths and stubbly chins, as if half their beards had gone on vacation. Mimi Mitchum was sitting in a chair watching every move they were making, which was none.

"Come here," she said, beckoning behind her back. I approached. Mimi's hair looked very similar to her husband's. When this was over, I wanted to go look at a real lawn for a change. "These three men," Mimi said, "are suspects in a recent theft. Last night, Polly Partial received a shipment of twenty blueberry pies. This morning she counted them and came up short."

"How many are missing?" I asked.

"Last night she had twenty," Harvey said, shutting the station door, "and today she counted zero. So at least eighteen are missing."

"At least," I agreed.

"Polly Partial saw a man in a red coat loading pies into a van marked with a French horn," Mimi said. "These three brothers run the only

French horn factory left in town, and their uniforms include red coats."

"Are you sure Ms. Partial is giving you an accurate account?" I asked, remembering how unreliable she had been as a witness recently.

"Sure we're sure," Mimi said, "but we're not sure which of the three is responsible."

I stepped forward and looked at the three men. The first was wearing a red coat. The second had a long work apron on, smudged here and there with black. The third wore a white T-shirt stained with blueberries.

"Don't look at me," said the first brother. "I'm innocent. Sure, I'm wearing a red coat, but I was nowhere near Partial Foods last night. I had to take over a shipment of French horns to the Devotee Symphony."

"Don't look at me either," said the man in the apron. "I was at the factory all day, polishing the last French horns we manufactured. We're closing down Tuesday, and we're all leaving town."

I turned my eyes to the blueberry-stained man and wondered if he would also proclaim his innocence. "I'd prefer you not look at me either," he said, and coughed a little.

"Now, maybe it's just because I'm tired," Harvey Mitchum said, scratching his head. "I admit that Mimi and I stayed up very late watching a double feature of scary movies."

"Something with zombies in the winter," Mimi said, "and something with giant bugs. We were scared out of our minds, and we've been exhausted all day. But this crime has stumped us, Snicket."

"Particularly Mimi," Harvey said.

"Particularly *you*," Mimi retorted.

"Particularly the way you snore," Harvey said.

"Particularly the way you drip-dry your socks in the bathroom," Mimi said.

"Those socks are part of my uniform, Mimi. If they're not clean, the law won't be clean."

"I wear police socks, too," Mimi said, "but I dry them in the machine."

"Perhaps," I said, before their argument took up the rest of my day, "I could question each of the suspects."

"Ask them anything you want," Harvey said with a dismissive gesture, like he was too tired to care about truth and justice and wanted to go home and watch some more giant bugs. In some ways, I could hardly blame him. It is more interesting to watch giant bugs and whatever they might do in a scary movie than to solve a minor and unimaginative crime. I looked at the three ragged men. All they wanted was to make French horns, and now they were in a jail cell in a town that was twisting itself into knots like the very instrument they manufactured. What will happen to them, I wondered, but it was not the question I asked.

I turned to the first brother. "Who is your favorite French writer?"

"Alain-Fournier," the man said, fiddling with one of the buttons on his red coat.

I turned to the second brother. "Who is your favorite jazz saxophonist?"

"Harry Carney," the man replied, brushing off his apron.

I turned to the third man. "And you," I asked. "What is your favorite food?"

The man shrugged his shoulders and gave a sigh of resignation, a phrase which here means he gave up. Perhaps he felt guilty, or perhaps he had also stayed up too late, scared or worried, and did not have the energy to be as clever as some other criminals I had encountered. It was a moment before he spoke, but "Blueberry pies" is what he said.

I turned to the Mitchums, who glared back at me, impatient and tired as the law itself. "I've solved the case," I told them.

• • •

The conclusion to "Three Suspects" is filed under "Very Obvious," page 245.

VANISHED MESSAGE.

It was another average morning with S. Theodora Markson in the Far East Suite. We were having a continental breakfast. In most cases, "continental breakfast" is a phrase which means "plenty of pastries and cereal, along with juice and coffee or tea." In my case, it meant just cereal, but we didn't have any bowls, so Theodora had simply poured a helping of Schoenberg Cereal onto the bureau, and I picked up the grainy flakes one by one and dipped them into the open milk carton. It felt like something an ant would do, although at least an ant has a colony of comrades for companionship. I just had my chaperone and her wild, enormous hair, which this morning had not one but two hairbrushes stuck in the back. I did not know if they were stuck there on purpose or by accident, and thinking about that made my morning seem even more ridiculous than it already was.

"Eat up, Snicket," Theodora was saying. "It says here on the back of the box that growing boys should have eleven servings of necessary nutrients per day."

"I've counted sixty-eight servings," I said.

"A single flake is not a serving, Snicket."

"It feels like one if you have to pinch it between your fingers and dip it into a carton of milk."

"A rug feels like a lion, but that doesn't mean you can ride it."

"What does that mean?"

"Think about it, Snicket."

"I *am* thinking about it. Nobody rides lions."

"That's not the point."

"What is the point?"

"You have to figure some things out yourself, Snicket. I can't spoon-feed you everything."

"I wish you'd spoon-feed me breakfast," I said. "This feels like it's taking forever."

"A rug feels like—"

There was a knock on the door before she could try to teach me the lesson again. The only rug that feels like a lion is made of lion.

"Who is it?" I asked, swallowing one last flake.

"Mail for Mr. Lemony Snicket," said a deep voice from behind the door.

"We can hear perfectly well that you're male," Theodora said. "But *which* male? We can't just let any man or boy into this room."

"An envelope, not the opposite of female," said the voice. "It's special delivery. I must put it directly in Mr. Snicket's hands."

I had been curious about the mail delivery

in Stain'd-by-the-Sea. It surprised me that the fading town still had a working postal service, and the speedy delivery of a mysterious package was an important part of my biggest case. I was very interested in seeing a postman at last, but it was Theodora who opened the door, and her enormous hair blocked my view, so I only saw a white-gloved hand reaching toward me, as if through a wild bush growing hairbrushes, and in an instant the envelope was in my hand and the door was shut again.

"Let me see that," Theodora said.

"It's addressed to me," I said, looking at the envelope. "I will read it in my morning bath."

"As your chaperone," my chaperone said, "I have a right to inspect all of your correspondence. You should have paid more attention during your training at headquarters."

"I'm sure headquarters would be shocked to hear that a chaperone plans on inspecting her apprentice while he's bathing," I said, and shut the door quickly. Threatening nudity is a powerful way to be left alone, and alone is the best way to do certain important tasks. Reading a mysterious letter certainly counted as important, I thought, sitting on the edge of the tub.

The envelope had my name on it in the wavering letters of a failing typewriter, and below it were the name and address of the Lost Arms. There was no return address, but the postmark told me the letter came from the city. There were many people in the city, of course, but I hoped that this letter brought me news of my sister, who was not only in the city but in a heap of trouble besides. But the letter was about another matter entirely.

Dear Mr. Snicket,

I have heard of your noble work and write to ask you a favor. I was recently in your town studying the Yamgraz. One afternoon I needed a

*break, so I took a walk to the Swinster Pharmacy
and sat at the counter, enjoying a tangerine soda
and writing postcards to various acquaintances
in the city. Most of the messages I wrote were
just friendly greetings, but on one postcard I
wrote a very important message. My plan was
to mail them at Stain'd Station, before I caught
my train home. But when I went to mail them,
my important message was gone. I believe I left
it at the soda counter, but the pharmacy hasn't
answered the phone, although I called either two
or three times. Mr. Snicket, I implore you to help
by finding this postcard and mailing it to the
recipient. "Implore" means "beg," by the way.
Because of the importance of the message, I ask
you to look only at the picture side, which shows
Blotto the Octopus, a character from a comic strip
that I understand used to run in the newspaper.
It's very important. I mean this sincerely.*

Sincerely,

Lois Dressing

I frowned at the letter and decided to skip my morning bath. I wondered if Theodora would notice. I wondered what kind of crucial information Ms. Dressing put on a postcard, which anyone can read, and while I was wondering, I wondered what in the world "Yamgraz" was. It can be frustrating when someone tells you the definition of a word you know, such as "implore," but not one you don't. It induces a state of discomfiture.

I told Theodora, who was brushing her hair with a third brush, that I needed some fresh air to go with my necessary nutrients, and I walked out of the Lost Arms onto the streets of Stain'd-by-the-Sea. The Swinster Pharmacy, I knew, was a building with a mysterious reputation in a part of town known as Flounder Ponds. Perhaps there had once been ponds and perhaps they'd been full of flounder, a fish shaped like it had been stepped on. Now the whole neighborhood looked stepped on, with only a few struggling businesses left open and a lot of empty houses. It was remarkable, I thought, how many neighborhoods were named after the things that used to be there before the neighborhood came along and changed the neighborhood.

I found the Swinster Pharmacy easily enough, even though I'd never been there. It looked like all mysterious buildings look when you approach them. It's difficult to describe, but imagine a creature, heavy and enormous, sleeping in great, loud breaths with its eyes closed. The eyes are the windows of the mysterious building. Now imagine that you must not wake it up. My hands were a little nervous on the door handle, and when I walked inside, the door closed behind me with a faint hiss I didn't care for.

The place was flyblown, a word which here means "squalid," a word which here means I wanted to leave immediately. The floor was very dark and the ceiling was very low. The windows had curtains that looked half-eaten. There were shelves of vitamins, painkillers, and other cures for ailments, but all the jars and bottles looked sticky and bruised. There was a rack of books I wouldn't read if you begged me, and along the far wall was the counter where Lois Dressing said she'd enjoyed a tangerine soda. It was very dusty, with padded seats ripped here and there and lonely striped linoleum that looked like it also wanted to leave immediately. I couldn't imagine enjoying anything there, let alone something tangerine-flavored.

"Hello?" I asked.

"Hello," a voice replied, so close I jumped. What I'd thought was some tubes of wrapping paper turned out to be the legs of an extremely tall man. He was as tall as three tall things stacked up on top of each other, with a white jacket with faint, tall stripes that made him look taller. His face was pale and old, and he either was wearing an unusual hat or his head fit neatly into one of the pharmacy's light fixtures.

"Are you ill?" the man asked.

"No," I said. "I'm Lemony Snicket. Are you Swinster?"

"There is no Swinster," said the man.

"I'm here to help a woman who was in here recently."

"Is she ill?"

"I hope not," I said. "She has troubles enough. She was in here recently and left an important postcard behind."

"I found no postcard."

"She tried to get ahold of you, but you didn't answer the phone."

"The phone is ill," said the man.

"Do you remember her, at least? She had a tangerine soda. Dressing was her name."

The man gave me a slow, tall blink, and then nodded. I watched carefully. It wasn't a hat. "Slightly," he said. "I don't pay much attention to people unless they're ill. She asked directions to Stain'd Station and I told her. But then she looked at her book and hurried out the door in the opposite direction."

"Did you happen to notice the name of the book?"

The man shrugged his shoulders. I almost expected to hear the ceiling crack. "The cover had a virus on it," he said.

"A virus?"

"Possibly a bacteria. It made the book look ill."

"And the woman didn't leave anything here?"

"A few coins, to pay for the soda."

"Nothing else?"

"A few more coins, as a tip."

"Do you mind if I look around?"

He said no, but it was me who minded. The

Swinster Pharmacy was a creepy place to look around, and I knew I wasn't going to find anything, and I didn't. There was nothing on the counter, behind it, or near it or far from it. There was nothing anywhere. I didn't even know what Blotto the Octopus looked like.

The door hissed behind me again as I left, and I wondered if there was anything more I could do. I did not know Lois Dressing and felt a little put out that she had written me out of the blue and sent me on a search that was none of my business. But "put out" is a phrase which here means "troubled," and I knew the feeling of being put out by a crucial, missing item. My biggest case revolved around an item that kept disappearing and reappearing all over town. I decided to go to the train station, the only other place I knew Ms. Dressing had been, and looked up at the street sign so I might figure out which way to go.

YAMGRAZ DRIVE

I looked at it a minute. Sometimes when you encounter a new word, you begin to see it everywhere. A mystery is solved with a story, but there was something about Lois Dressing's story that I hadn't understood from the beginning. Yamgraz Drive took me in the direction of the library, the long way around, and my sixty-nine servings of necessary nutrients hadn't provided me with enough fuel to make the journey comfortably. I was tempted to stop at Hungry's for a sandwich. My associate Jake Hix made good sandwiches. I decided they were so good that one could be a reward for a job well done rather than a break from a job not yet completed.

Dashiell Qwerty, Stain'd-by-the-Sea's only librarian and a splendid one, was busy behind his desk. At first glance, I thought he was swatting moths, continuing a fierce battle between librarian and insect I had witnessed with every visit to the library, but when I looked closely, he was holding a book open and shaking it vigorously over his desk. It looked like he was encouraging the book to spit up something it was choking on.

"Good morning, Qwerty."

"Good morning," Qwerty replied. "Don't mind me. A certain reader in town always leaves things behind in the books she borrows. Last month I found two shed snakeskins and a doily that was quite finely made."

I was barely listening. There were enough lost small objects in my life. I had been in the library long enough to know where the best dictionary was, and I told Qwerty I needed it and he told me to help myself, but in a moment I needed more help than myself could give me.

"Qwerty, it's not here."

"What's not here?" Qwerty said, coming out from behind his desk.

"A word I need defined. It's not in the dictionary."

"Did you use the good one?"

"Of course, Qwerty," I said, reminding myself to ask him sometime why he kept mediocre dictionaries on the shelf.

"What's the word?"

"Yamgraz."

Qwerty smiled like I'd given him the right answer. "Put the dictionary away," he said. "That's a proper noun."

"And what does it properly mean?"

"The Yamgraz were the people who lived in this area first."

"Before Stain'd-by-the-Sea, you mean?"

"Oh, yes, long before. The Yamgraz lived on the shoreline, near where the Clusterous Forest is now. They were shellfishing people, I believe, who ate the innards of the oyster and used the shells as tools and castanets."

"What happened to them?" I asked.

173

"We live here now," Qwerty said, and he sounded a little sad about it. "Fishing boats arrived, then ink was discovered, and then the railway, which started transporting oysters to the city for fancy parties. Look here."

The librarian had led me to the local history section, with which I was also familiar. The books there had taken me back in time through Stain'd-by-the-Sea's mysterious history, to the days of fierce battles and troubling myths, but I'd never gone as far back as the Yamgraz, who were now nothing more than a street sign in a town that was hardly much more than nothing at all. I stared at the spines of the books and took one out immediately. I shouldn't have been surprised at the cover. An oyster shell can look like a virus, particularly if you are looking at it from a great height.

"Anything more I can get you?" Qwerty asked me with a smile.

"No," I said, looking down at the spine. "This book should cough up what I'm looking for."

•   •   •

The conclusion to "Vanished Message" is filed under "Message Received," page 249.

TROUBLESOME GHOST.

I woke up early and uncomfortable under my heavy blanket. Outside the window the morning was gray, and the air felt like a heavy blanket. At the other end of the Far East Suite was the figure of S. Theodora Markson, snoring in bed. She looked like a heavy blanket. When everything reminds you of a heavy blanket, you are probably going to have a grumpy day. I grumped out of bed and put on my clothes. They felt like a heavy blanket.

I knew one of Theodora's meager breakfasts was not going to improve my mood, so I walked downstairs and nodded at Prosper Lost on my way out of the Lost Arms. He nodded back, or maybe the proprietor of the hotel was asleep. Stain'd-by-the-Sea once had a great number of restaurants, most of them specializing in seafood. With the sea drained away, the seafood was in very scarce supply, so now most of the town's restaurants specialized in being closed and boarded up. But Hungry's, where my associate Jake Hix cooked up marvelous things behind the counter, was still around, and I thought a Hix breakfast might improve my morning. I took the short walk through the quiet streets. The morning fog hung slow and thick around the streetlights. I probably don't need to tell you what that reminded me of.

I expected to be Hungry's only customer, but when I walked in, Jake was serving up a plate of banana waffles to a worried-looking man in overalls that looked worried, too. If you've ever had a good banana waffle, you know it's nothing to worry about, and Jake's waffles were very good. His secret was that he caramelized the bananas first, although there's no reason to tell him who you learned that from.

"Good morning, Snicket. My waffle iron's still hot, if you're interested."

"I'm definitely interested," I said.

"And a cup of tea to go with it?"

"I'm interested in that, too."

"And a ghost story? Would you be interested in that?"

I just gave him a look. Everyone's interested in ghost stories. If you ask if anyone wants to hear a ghost story, no one is going to say, "No thanks, I'd rather just sit here," and neither did I. Jake gestured to his other customer, and the worried-looking man shook my hand, and when he was done with his bite of waffle, told me his name.

"Hans Mann," he said.

"Lemony Snicket," I said.

"You're not from around here," the man said.

"Snicket's only been in town a little while," Jake said, busy with bananas at the stove, "but he's helped out a lot of people."

"I wish he'd help out my mother," Hans said, "but I'm afraid it's too late now."

Jake tilted the sizzling bananas into a bowl of batter. "Hans used to work at the Stain'd Playhouse," he said. "He built all the sets for the big productions, and Old Lady Mann ran the box office."

"We put on some terrific shows back then," Hans said wistfully. "We had a huge pirate ship with all the rigging for *Shiver Me Timbers*. Sally Murphy rose to the ceiling on invisible wires when she played the title role in *Mother of Icarus*. We even had a train wreck onstage when we performed *Look Out for That Train Wreck*."

"I remember that," Jake said, whisking briskly.

"I could never figure out how you split that passenger car in two every night."

"The whole thing was held together with chains," Hans explained. "When the actor playing the cowboy shouted 'I wonder what's taking Margery so long,' Billy Becker and I would give the apparatus a good tug and it would split apart. The chains were hidden behind the train car so the audience couldn't see them, and after the shepherd discovered his identical twin in the last scene, the curtain would come down and we'd push the two halves of the train car back together for the next performance."

"And now you're doing a play about ghosts?" I asked.

"I don't build sets anymore," Hans said with a sigh. "When the Playhouse closed down, I moved to the city and found work in a staple gun factory."

"Most of the actors and stagehands have left town," Jake said to me. "Billy Becker and Sally

Murphy are the only ones still in Stain'd-by-the-Sea. Billy lives in an old shack in what used to be the Anchovy District, and spends his time trying to catch rats in an old pillowcase, and you know what Sally Murphy's up to."

"I do indeed," I said grimly, thinking of my biggest case.

"Becker and Murphy aren't the only ones," Hans said. "My mother's still here. She's old and her legs ache and she hardly ever leaves the house, but she's still around."

"What does she do all day?" Jake asked.

"Reads," Hans replied, "plays the harmonium, and maintains the fish scale mosaics."

"I thought she donated those to a museum someplace," Jake said. "Those mosaics are worth a fortune."

"She wants them in her house until the day she no longer lives there," Hans said, "but I'm afraid that day has come. I drove in from the city today to get my mother to come live with me. It's nothing like our grand home here in Stain'd-by-the-Sea, but there's a small spare room waiting for her in my apartment, and the staple gun factory has agreed to let her work part-time in the Customer Complaints Department."

"Listening to people complain about their staple guns can't be as fun as playing the harmonium," I said.

"You got that right, brother," Hans said, "but you can't always have the life you want most. I wish my mother could live in the Mann mansion forever, but she's too frightened of my father's ghost to live out here by herself anymore."

"Waffles are ready," Jake said, and gave me mine. I dug in. It was a good time to eat, now that we were at the ghost part of the ghost story, although any time would have been a good time to dig into these waffles. Hix had put a thin layer of whipped cream, real whipped cream that wasn't too sweet, in between them, making each bite crisp and light, the opposite of a heavy blanket and the heavy sigh Hans gave me as he continued his story.

"A few weeks ago," he said, "my mother woke up in the middle of the night to a loud noise coming from the East Wing. She put on her slippers and walked downstairs to see what it was. She told me it sounded clanky and rattly, but when she got there, the noise stopped, and she didn't see anything unusual in the sitting room, the game room, or the solarium. Thinking it was her imagination, she returned to her room, but she was kept up all night by a sinister muttering that was coming from under the bed. She turned on the lights and searched everywhere but couldn't find anything, even though the muttering continued all night, along with squeaks and scrapes that lasted until dawn. When she finally went down the west staircase to have her morning tea in the morning tea room, she was a wreck, and when she went back upstairs to change out of her robe, she found that the chest at the foot of her bed had been opened and all of its contents thrown around the room."

"What were its contents?" Jake asked. "Was there anything valuable inside the chest?"

"It was nothing but heavy blankets," replied Hans.

"Hmm," I said.

"You need maple syrup, Snicket?" Jake asked.

"No thanks," I said. I never need maple syrup. I can't shake the feeling that it's like drinking the blood of a tree. "What happened next, Hans?"

"What happened next was the same thing the next night," Hans said, "and the next and the next and the next. Clanking in some distant part of the house, and then muttering and scraping under the bed."

"I'm surprised Old Lady Mann didn't sleep in a different room," Jake said. "There must be a dozen bedrooms in that place."

"Seventeen," Hans said. "We used to host

visiting theater troupes when they came through town. Some of the bedrooms have been closed up for years, but even when my mother tried sleeping in those rooms, the noises followed her, and there were things thrown around every morning." He pushed his plate away and faced me. "Hix knows my mother," he said, "but you don't, Snicket. So let me tell you that she is tough as nails. She doesn't frighten easily. In fifty years of local theater she's seen too many crazy actors and elaborate productions to be troubled by nonsense. So when she told me she was frightened, I was worried, but now she's panicked and I'm frantic."

I put down my fork. It is not polite to talk to frantic people with one's mouth full of whipped cream. "Was there something specific that made her panic?" I asked.

Hans nodded. "Last night, she says, she finally saw the ghost who was responsible for all the disturbances."

"There are many things that could be responsible instead of ghosts," I said.

"Right again, brother," Hans said with a nod. "I don't believe in ghosts, and my mother never did either. But last night she told me she saw the ghost of my father floating outside her bedroom window. That's on the fifth floor! No person could climb up all that way!"

"Most people couldn't," I agreed, "but some people could. I went to school with a few of them. I bet there's even a windowsill they could stand on."

"It's too narrow," Hans said, "and too crumbly. But my mother said she saw my father there, clear as day in the middle of the night—a floating, fluttering specter with a dark and shadowy face."

"A shadowy face," I repeated. "Then how could your mother be sure who it was?"

"Because she was married to him for thirty-seven years," Hans said. "You could recognize your husband, even if it was dark out."

"The whole town could recognize him," Jake said. "He was famous in Stain'd-by-the-Sea. He made those mosaics we were talking about."

"He was in a few of the Playhouse shows, too," Hans said. "I remember my sister worked all night on his costume for *The Man Who Looked Somewhat Like Winston Churchill* before she joined the air force. But now it's my father's ghost flying around out there, my mother says. But it doesn't really matter if it's a real ghost or not. I'm taking my mother back to the city."

"Not so fast," Jake said, and pointed his spatula at me. "I bet Snicket can solve this mystery just by asking a question or two. Am I wrong, Snicket?"

"What makes these bananas taste so good?" I asked.

Hix frowned, and I guess I deserved a frown. I was showing off a little.

"I caramelize them," Jake said, "but that's a professional secret."

"It's no secret that the world is full of secrets," I said. "I guess we'd better go over to the Mann mansion and uncover one or two."

"You're welcome to talk to my mother," Hans said, "but I told you everything she told me."

"It's not your mother I want to talk to," I said, and pushed my plate away with a sigh. "In a way I feel sorry for the guy. You were right, Hans. You can't always have the life you want most. And even if the mosaics go to a museum, a mansion is a much better home than an old shack in the former Anchovy District."

• • •

The conclusion to "Troublesome Ghost" is filed under "Train Wreck," page 253.

FIGURE IN FOG.

Sometimes you are suspicious because of something, and sometimes you are suspicious because of nothing. This incident began in the library, where I could find nothing good to read. This was suspicious. Stain'd-by-the-Sea's library was not particularly big, but it was one of those libraries that seemed to grow bigger every time I visited. Thanks to the librarian, Dashiell Qwerty, the shelves kept offering books that again and again turned out to be just what

I needed at the time. But this afternoon what I needed was to go outside. Nothing told me this. I just shut the fifth book I'd tried, and knew. The book had begun with a brute of a man who attacked a little girl, and then felt bad about it and offered her family a huge sum of money that he'd stolen from a famous scientist. If that didn't interest me, it was time to leave the library.

Outside it was foggy, which was also suspicious. The sea had been drained away from the shores of Stain'd-by-the-Sea so Ink Inc., the biggest company in town, could chase the last few remaining octopi and keep the ink industry alive for just a little longer. Usually, if there's no sea there's no fog, but nobody had told the fog this. From time to time a thick gray mist spread out over the empty seascape, dribbling over bridges that had once curved over the rippling waters, and wrapping itself around Offshore Island, where a bell still rang from a tower sometimes, and that was suspicious, too.

"Leaving so soon?" asked a voice behind me, and I turned around to see Dashiell Qwerty shooing a moth out of his library. "I should think on a day like this you'd want to stay inside and read a book, not wander around town."

"It *is* a little miserable out there," I agreed, gesturing toward the lawn, "but it's interesting, too. I thought you could only have fog near a body of water."

"Oh, no," Qwerty said, frowning at the departing moth. "Many marshes or unusually damp valleys create enough moisture for fog."

"But there aren't any marshes around here, are there?"

"There are not."

"And the valleys are not particularly damp."

"They are not."

"So the whole thing is suspicious."

Qwerty cocked his head at me. "The whole thing?" he repeated.

"The fog," I said. "The vanished sea, the

living forest of seaweed, the island and its bell, the thefts, the disappearances, the kidnappings, the mysteries, the puzzling pieces of a shadowy and fiendish plot with an equally shadowy and perhaps even more fiendish villain." I paused, not knowing how much of the story I should tell him. Librarians are generally trustworthy people, but part of a librarian's job is to make information available to everyone, and this was information I felt should be kept secret. "All the strange encounters," I finished, "and all the troubling incidents I seem to find in this town."

"Do you find them, Snicket? Or do they find you?"

"I don't know what you mean."

"Look at it this way, Snicket," Qwerty said as the fog kept rolling across the grass. "To a stranger in town, such as yourself, Stain'd-by-the-Sea is full of suspicious incidents. But to the people of Stain'd-by-the-Sea, you're a suspicious incident yourself. You arrived out of the blue and live in a hotel suite with an adult who seems to be neither your parent nor your guardian. You ask a lot of questions about anything and everything, and anyone and everyone has questions about you. There are rumors you're part of a secret organization. There are rumors you are in charge of an important investigation. But nobody really seems to have the foggiest notion what you're up to." The librarian sighed, a great billowy sigh that went perfectly with the fog. "What are you up to, Snicket?"

"I couldn't find anything good to read," I said, "so I thought I'd take a walk."

"Good luck," Qwerty replied.

"With my walk?"

"With the whole thing," Qwerty said, and gave me a wave as he walked back into the library. Conversations with Dashiell Qwerty often brought me more questions than answers, but many conversations with librarians are like that. If you're a librarian, questions are good for business.

I walked down the stairs, which had once been impressive, and away from the building, which had once been City Hall, but I stopped halfway across the lawn, right near the ruins of what had once been an important statue. I stopped for a reason.

There was a figure in the fog.

The figure looked about my size, perhaps a little taller. The figure was just a little ways away, facing me, with its arms straight down and its legs slightly apart, like it was about to move. But it wasn't moving. It wasn't doing anything, and that's what seemed suspicious.

"Hello?" I said.

The figure seemed to nod. That seemed suspicious, too, although I had to remind myself that there was nothing wrong with nodding. Still, I wondered why the figure hadn't replied with "Hello" or "Good afternoon" or "Foggy out today, isn't it?" or even "Lemony Snicket, you didn't recognize me, did you? It's me, Such-

and-such, your associate, and I've found a place in Stain'd-by-the-Sea that makes very good root beer floats and I'd like to buy you one." Instead it had said nothing, and instead it had done nothing, and now it still was saying nothing and doing nothing, and all these nothings made me suspicious, so at last, when it stopped doing nothing and began to walk, I decided to follow.

I've said before that the trick to following someone without getting caught is to follow somebody who doesn't know they're being followed, but of course if you have no idea who the person is you're following, you have no idea if they know you're following them, and so you have no idea if you're going to be caught or not. If you think you might be caught at something, you should have an excuse ready, so I decided that if the figure confronted me, I would say I was just trying to find the Lost Arms and got lost in the fog. It wasn't a great excuse, but I couldn't think of a better one. In any case, if the figure knew it was being followed, it didn't do anything about it. It kept walking, and I kept following, about half a block behind. I still couldn't tell anything about the figure. I couldn't tell if it was male or female, child or adult, stranger or associate. All I knew was that it was suspicious, although I thought of what Qwerty had said, and realized maybe I was the suspicious one. After all, I was following somebody. The figure was just walking.

It turned out to be a long walk, through many streets and alleys in many neighborhoods of Stain'd-by-the-Sea. We walked without rhyme or reason, a phrase which here means every which way, and although we passed many places which were familiar to me, the route was an unfamiliar one. At times it seemed we were going in circles, or taking the long way around or perhaps a shortcut that had never occurred to me, or maybe we were traveling along a very definite path, taking the shortway or a longcut that had occurred to me many times, as the town was so foggy and empty that I was growing confused. Confusion is not good if you are already suspicious. Suspicion means you think something is going to happen. Confusion means you don't know what it is. If something is going to happen and you don't know what it is, you begin to ask yourself more and more questions and get more and more suspicious and confused.

Sure enough, as the figure led me through Stain'd-by-the-Sea, I asked myself more and more questions about suspicious incidents I had recently encountered.

We passed a boarded-up window that had once been smashed, and I thought of the Big Bad Brick Gang and their burglaries, and I wondered about all of the closed-up businesses, and where all the shopkeepers had gone when their stores had vanished.

We walked by a stationery store, and I thought of the staple gun factory and Hans and the rattling chains in his mother's house, and I wondered about theatrical productions, fish scale mosaics, and other lost creations of the residents of Stain'd-by-the-Sea.

We crossed the road that led to the office of the Doctors Sobol, and I thought of Oliver and his two pairs of glasses, and I wondered how to keep something as fragile and valuable as a rare newt safe in such a ragged and desperate place as Stain'd-by-the-Sea, or any amusement park.

We passed Hungry's, and I thought of the voice coming out of the walkie-talkie, and I wondered why the guy who came into town once a month for steak frites lived in a condominium just a few blocks from the diner.

We rounded Homily Hill, and I thought about the sled race and the photograph and the party at Mr. Willow's home, and I wondered about a person who had once loved a man enough to get married and despised him enough to frame him for theft.

We walked around a deep, dark hole in the ground, and I thought of Marguerite, the minor and the miner, and I wondered about her mother, who had left her beloved portraits on the walls but was nowhere to be found.

We walked by Moray Wheels, and I thought about the missing dog and the mechanic named Jackie and I wondered about a grandfather who liked to joyride, and a grandchild who liked to repair automobiles, and how long they could continue to live in a town that was going nowhere.

We passed an abandoned band shell, where brass bands must have performed in better times, and I thought of the French horn factory and the three brothers in the Mitchums' jail, and I wondered how many people in Stain'd-by-the-Sea were hungry enough to steal.

We walked by a chain-link fence with a hole

in it, and I thought of Randall and the drifters and the stolen spoon, and I wondered how desperate you would have to be to live on the outskirts of a town that was almost gone.

We passed the Swinster Pharmacy, and I thought of Lois Dressing and the postcard, and wondered about the Yamgraz, and what vanished people had come even before them.

We walked by Cozy's, and I thought of the twins and the failing rocking chair business and wondered why some people believed in things like demons, and if they were right to do so.

We passed Black Cat Coffee, and I wondered if a small boy was safe and sound. But I also wondered about someone else, a mysterious figure who was the reason I'd stopped by Black Cat Coffee that day and any other day. Maybe the mysterious figure is the mysterious figure, I thought to myself. She's the type who might nod, rather than return a greeting. She's the type who might lead me all around town. She's

the type you might end up following, Snicket, even though you'd be suspicious about where she might lead you. The figure got farther and farther ahead of me until I found myself calling her name into the fog.

Maybe the figure was Ellington Feint and maybe it wasn't, but suddenly I knew one thing for certain about the figure, and that was that the figure was gone.

I looked this way and that, the way you do when you are alone and hope you aren't, or when you aren't but hope you are. I thought I heard footsteps in the fog, but I didn't have the foggiest notion where they were coming from or what they were up to, or even if they were suspicious after all. Just because you think it's suspicious doesn't mean it is. Think of what Qwerty said, about all the people in Stain'd-by-the-Sea who are suspicious of you, just because you're a stranger in town and they don't have the foggiest notion of what you're up to.

And then I heard a sound—a person's voice calling a single word.

I could not tell where exactly it was coming from or what exactly it was saying, and I didn't know whose voice it was. I didn't even know if it sounded familiar. The villain I was facing, in my biggest case, had the skill of imitating anyone's voice. It could be him imitating someone. It could be someone he was imitating. It could be someone else imitating someone else. It was another mystery, another suspicious incident, or perhaps it was nothing. The voice called out again, a single word I could not quite catch, like something in a book that's difficult to understand, or written in fading ink.

I stood in the fog and wondered what to do next. Wherever I went in town, I found questions I had to ask, no matter how wrong and no matter how suspicious the answers might be. You're going to keep asking questions, Snicket, I thought to myself. You'll keep searching for the right answers even if the questions are wrong. The voice called out again, and I took a deep breath and followed it into the fog.

•   •   •

The conclusion to "Figure in Fog" is filed under "Shouted Word,"

page 257.

Sub-file B:
CONCLUSIONS.

Black Paint. Deep Mine. Dishonest Salesman. Back-
seat. Loud Dog. Quiet Street. Through the Window.
Beneath the Street. Homemade Furniture. Small Court-
yard. Twenty-Five Guests. Missing Pets. Small Sound.
Large Meal. Chalked Name. Other Name. Panicked
Feet. Sand and Shore. Very Obvious. Poor Joke.
Message Received. Message Recorded. Train Wreck.
Nervous Wreck. Shouted Word. Last Word.

BLACK PAINT.

As Marguerite had noticed, the paintings were falling "too neatly"—because they weren't falling at all. Dagmar was taking them down in order to steal the nails which held the paintings up. Marguerite's father had melted down the mined gold and formed it into nails—a perfect way to keep his gold safe and hidden. After the first painting fell, Dagmar must have noticed what the nails were made of—probably when the black paint chipped off—and concocted a plan to steal the Gracq gold, nail by nail. This was all explained over a late breakfast of very fluffy eggs while Dagmar was arrested.

In prison, there is no polka music.

DEEP MINE.

What Dagwood failed to realize was that the mysterious sound from the mine continued even after the electric equipment was turned off. Therefore the buzzing was of natural origin and the sack of spare batteries would have been useless. As with many suspicious incidents, the solution was to keep digging, which is why the shovels and notebooks were found by museum authorities the next morning.

DISHONEST SALESMAN.

The man by the side of the road said that the Amaranthine Newt might have hidden itself in the zinnias, which were yellow and orange, like the building's trim. But anyone who was not a herpetologist or a southpaw would guess that the Amaranthine Newt would be purple, not yellow, and thus not able to hide. The stranger was thus not a doorknob salesman but a thief who had left his car by the side of the road to pinch the newt while Oliver was gardening. Caught, he returned the stolen creature, and everything was back to normal, although Paperbag's disorder has not yet cleared up.

BACKSEAT.

The inside of a car would not have been warm enough to hatch reptile or amphibian eggs. As veterinarians, the Doctors Sobol would have known this, and would have smuggled the eggs in their coat pockets, which were likely lined with fur, or scaly skin. But Bertram found the coats hanging on the rack near the drafty window, so therefore it was the heated suitcase, stored near the stove, that contained the stolen items, which were returned immediately.

Many have described the taste of root beer, but that afternoon it tasted like justice.

LOUD DOG.

The Dugga Drills would have been easier for a stranger to steal than Lysistrata, as the dog would have barked at anyone she didn't recognize, while the drills would have kept quiet. But Lysistrata wouldn't have barked at Jackie's grandfather, who spent most of his time at Moray Wheels. A former race car driver, he was so eager to drive the Dilemma that he concocted a plot to get his grandchild away from the garage so he could take the car for a joyride. He hid

Lysistrata at the bowling alley, where the sounds of pins and bowling balls would have drowned out any panicked barking. Jackie's grandfather was indeed found driving the Dilemma and loving it almost as much as Lysistrata did. They both had their faces out the window, the better to feel the magical terror of rushing night air.

·

QUIET STREET.

Blotted Boulevard is a perfect place for a shadowy meeting by sinister cohorts working in secrecy, but so many organizations were using it that a sign-up sheet became necessary to reduce the chances of confusion, embarrassment, and duels. Violetta Frogg-Drifter turned out to be a fake name used only on such paperwork.

THROUGH THE WINDOW.

OFF-SBTS-USE stands for "Official Stain'd-by-the-Sea Use." The walkie-talkies were meant for the police, but Stew had swiped two from his parents, dropped one under the counter, and used the other in the bathroom, in an attempt to empty the diner and grab a fourth muffin. Once he said, "Don't just hang around the door," it was obvious he wasn't miles away, but close enough to see the person to whom he was talking.

Jake's next batch of muffins was pecan. He offered them on a sliding scale, a phrase which here means "free for Lemony Snicket, but not to be sold to Stew Mitchum under any circumstances."

BENEATH THE STREET.

"Drain-Leads-to-Sea" is a phrase which here means "a passageway ideal for small lizards and amphibians to travel to the Clusterous Forest." The noises in the echoey passageway would have carried to other underground structures, such as basements and mines.

HOMEMADE
FURNITURE.

People who share their pirate books might be sharing a crime as well. Kevin Old, son of the Boards shopkeeper, was in cahoots with Florence Smith, the daughter of the owner of Chrysanthemums. Florence wanted a bookshelf, and Kevin wanted a sword, so they concocted a story about a gang and even broke an extra window to put people off the trail.

SMALL COURTYARD.

The key was in the cobblestones. If they could be pushed aside by the growth of small plants, they likely wouldn't hold up against violent animal life when used in the construction of clinics and schools. Both Dagwood and Violetta would have known this from their father, a geologist and former travel agent who lived in the same neighborhood.

TWENTY-FIVE GUESTS.

Smogface would have no way of knowing about Ashbery, the one-eared dog, unless he had been at the drifters' camp, as Randall did not bring his dog into town when he was working. Wiley was collecting spoons monogrammed with each letter of the alphabet, in order to have the twenty-six-guest dinner parties he believed were well-bred. He begrudgingly handed the *R* over before throwing his visitor out. On his ear.

MISSING PETS.

Armadale's lizards were transported in a large tank originally designed for amphibians, large enough to hold the reptiles comfortably but small enough to fit into the trunk of a car. When confronted, Mrs. Flammarion admitted as much and returned the keys and wig.

SMALL SOUND.

A hollow metal space will amplify small noises, such as the breathing of a young, frightened boy. Drumstick was hiding in the garbage can, dirty but grateful and seriously considering becoming a vegetarian.

LARGE MEAL.

"A simple sauce of unsalted butter" was flatly impossible, as any good butcher knows that preparing the meat of lizards and amphibians requires a great deal of salt, easily gathered from land that was once the ocean floor. Local diners expressed relief and gratitude, and the stew has never been advertised again.

CHALKED NAME.

Mrs. Willow was not holding her husband's sled, which would have been marked with the number four. She was holding her own, unmarked sled. She was the thirteenth sledder, joining the race in secret and stealing the painting in order to frame her husband and run away with the lawn mower technician. Ms. Mallahan and Mr. Snicket notified the authorities in town, but Mr. Willow had escaped from prison some time before with a skeleton key. Did his locksmith wife regret framing him? Or did he escape of his own accord? Anyone with further information should contact us through the publisher.

OTHER NAME.

The reverse side of the newspaper had an article on party refreshments, including The Salty Mess, a recipe containing caviar, salted meat, and six slices of honeydew melon arranged into two initials. If the paper had been truly folded in half, the villain would have been warned either way.

PANICKED FEET.

Tatiana fell on the piers to give Treacle enough time to dash back to Cozy's, to give himself the appearance of innocence. But he had to work quickly to change out of the long, black coat and into his pajamas. He hid his long, bushy wig in the most convenient place—in the basket, where it blended in with the hairy dog. It would have worked, but when the dog was summoned the wig was revealed. After some conversation over tea, the twins agreed to get Tatiana out of her marriage through calm conversation rather than tricks with demons, though the mystery of why anyone likes rocking chairs remains to be solved.

SAND AND SHORE.

"What once was desert is water," the slogan said, but it did not mention what happened to what once was water. Three forgotten ships would have had more than enough rope on board to tow anything—or anyone—that heavy.

VERY OBVIOUS.

It was the third brother, of course. It's important to get a good night's rest.

POOR JOKE.

"Because blueberries are yummy," explained the young rabbi, and the entire congregation laughed and coughed nearly until sunrise.

MESSAGE RECEIVED.

Lois Dressing, sipping tangerine soda, had suddenly realized she was about to leave town with a library book on the Yamgraz, and hurried back to the library. In her haste, she left the postcard in the book, and by the time she was at Stain'd Station noticing its absence, Qwerty had put the book back on the shelf. Luckily, no one had checked it out in the interim, possibly because of the unsightly cover design.

Dear Headquarters,

If you are receiving this postcard it means Mr. Snicket has passed the test and is therefore progressing nicely as an apprentice in our organization. Please note the dated postmark for our records and make a note in the Snicket file.

> *With all due respect,*
> *L.D.*

The other side depicts a tedious joke starring an octopus. It is almost impossible to look at only one side of a postcard.

MESSAGE RECORDED.

Minutes from meeting at Stain'd Station:

> **T:** Good afternoon.
> **Q:** Good afternoon.
>
> **T:** Did you bring the castanets?
> **Q:** What?
>
> **T:** Are they in your hat? Give it to me.
> **Q:** What are you talking about? Leave my hat alone!

T: Wait, are you in a secret organization?

Q: Of course not.

T: My apologies. I thought you were someone else.

Q [?]: Who?

T: Nothing. Excuse me. Pardon me.
Good-bye.

TRAIN WRECK.

Billy Becker was a stagehand who helped Hans with some of the Stain'd Playhouse's spectacular effects. Tired of living in a shack, he came up with a few effects of his own, to scare Old Lady Mann out of town and leave the mansion empty for him to move into. The clanking sound was likely old chains left over from *Look Out for That Train Wreck*, and the "ghost" was simply Mr. Mann's old costume from *The Man Who Looked Somewhat Like Winston Churchill* strung up on the wires that lifted Sally Murphy to the ceiling, and the muttering and scuffling were rats trapped in pillowcases that Becker would then hide under the bed while Old Lady Mann was investigating some of the more distant noises. Mr. Becker was found hiding in a distant laundry room in the Mann mansion, and once confronted, confessed to his plan. Old Lady Mann took pity on her former coworker and agreed to let him stay in the East Wing, and now the only mysterious noises that come from the mansion are songs from old Playhouse musicals, sung in a very low voice with harmonium accompaniment.

NERVOUS WRECK.

In some instances, eliminating every other word from a speech in a play results in a secret message, as in this scene from *Mother of Icarus*:

Naucrate: ~~There~~ she ~~is~~, offering ~~nothing~~ more ~~to~~ Icarus's ~~report~~ card ~~at~~ school. ~~This~~ terrible ~~time~~ must ~~stop~~! I'm ~~looking~~ desperately ~~for~~ something—~~a~~ brilliant ~~message~~, perhaps!

SHOUTED WORD.

The conclusion to this mystery is still in progress, and our organization encourages further input by volunteers in the field.

LAST WORD.

"___ ___ ___ ___ ___ ___ ___ ___."

Sub-file III:
ALL THE WRONG
QUESTIONS

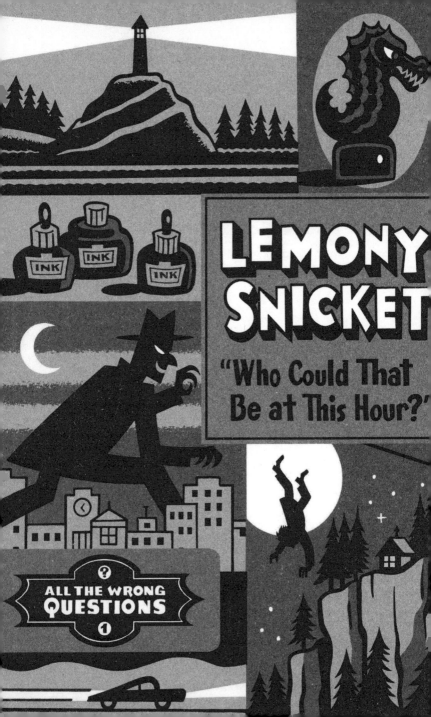

"Who Could That Be at This Hour?" is the first of Mr. Snicket's four-volume report, *All the Wrong Questions*, which details a case involving theft, kidnapping, strong coffee, fear of heights, honeydew melons, and murder. Excerpt below.

The screaming seemed to come from everyplace, echoing in the long, empty hallway. I thought I remembered a carpet on the floor when I had first entered the Sallis mansion, but I hadn't been paying much attention. The floor was bare now.

"The mansion is too big," I said. "We're going to have to split up."

"You want me to find whoever's screaming by myself?" Moxie asked.

"Get scared later," I told her, and hurried down the hallway and up a wide flight of stairs.

LEMONY SNICKET is older than you and should know better. He is responsible for *All the Wrong Questions,* as well as all the books in *A Series of Unfortunate Events.*

SETH appears innocent, but looks can be deceiving. He is the creator of *Palookaville, Clyde Fans,* and *The Great Northern Brotherhood of Canadian Cartoonists* and can be blamed for the art in *All the Wrong Questions.*